MOVIEMAKERS

KEITH LONG

ISBN: 979-8-218-44671-0

DEDICATION

To my lifelong friends Ben Skrivseth and Dan Ferraro, and to all who've collaborated with me in my video productions, especially my brother Dave—and in memory of Ted Larson, my college filmmaking professor.

"Hell, there are no rules here—we're trying to accomplish something."

-Thomas Edison

Co-inventor of the kinetograph in 1890, which is widely recognized as one of the world's first motion picture cameras.

ACKNOWLEDGMENTS

I first began writing *Moviemakers* in 2003. What a feeling to finally acknowledge those who have helped me to cross the finish line. A tremendous thanks to my wife and children for putting up with me and for all the fun and loving support throughout our adventures together. A huge thanks to my mom for her encouragement, and to those who contributed their expertise to this project, photographers Stephen Holdaway (VHS), Chepko Danil Vitalevich (Camcorder), Irham Setaki (Clapper), Clement Souchet (Lights), Aleah Keske for the cover design, and Alisha Nygaard for the editing.

I didn't know what I'd do with this story when I started all those years ago, but I guarantee that the cover design by Aleah Keske was not in my wildest dreams. THANK YOU Aleah!

Finally, readers need to know that without Alisha's input and expertise, *Moviemakers* would still be sitting in a Microsoft Word document unfinished. I had so much fun working with her on this story. THANK YOU Alisha!

"*Simon!* Why is there a hole in the wall where there used to be a pencil sharpener?" Mr. Larson whipped around and shouted toward the back of the classroom.

With a shake of his head and a helpless, blank stare in Simon's direction, our Media Arts teacher paused with his mouth agape, as if trying to formulate further admonishment. The class held its collective breath as we studiously observed our teacher for any signs that *our* shenanigans would be compromised. And then, like clockwork, our teacher's eyes returned to their default glaze, and he turned around and resumed writing on the chalkboard.

The class let out an audible sigh of relief. You see, we needed Mr. Larson's painfully slow chalkboard writing to give us time to finish our paper football Super Bowl matchup; an intense back and forth shootout, which everyone except Simon was watching. It's a game we played whenever our teachers turned their backs for long stretches of time. Mr. Larson's class was far and away the best because of how many uninterrupted games we could get in—a player could really get on a roll and build some momentum.

For this reason alone, Media Arts was easily my favorite subject—but I had at least three other reasons: (1) Media Arts was the only class that I shared with my best friends; (2) *and* the girl of my dreams; (3) finally, what made this class really stand out was that we would be graded on our ability to make a *movie* for our final project. *A movie!* Math, English, Science—none of those classes provided anything nearly as interesting and exciting as Mr. Larson's final assignment. My friends and I had seen so many movies and we had our hearts set on finally making one of our own—and if things worked out just right, we would get to be moviemakers for this assignment *together*.

But first, I wanted to dispatch the dweeb I was facing in the Super Bowl. As long as there was time on the clock and chalk in Mr. Larson's hand, paper football's top honors were as good as mine. Oh how Mr. Larson loved that chalkboard! He and that smooth, green surface were practically attached at the hip—or rather, *the belly*. If we were lucky enough to catch him on a particularly ambitious lesson plan, it was a foregone conclusion that all we would see from Mr. Larson would be his enormous backside. Plus, when he was hell bent on getting all those words on the board, he tended to lose track of his belly and it would slide along the lower half of the board, erasing all his freshly chalked handwriting in the process.

My guess was that Mr. Larson probably only taught us a single day's worth of material the entire year. His wonderful inability to *actually teach us* had provided my friends and me the chance to organize and play an entire sixteen game paper football season with a single-elimination tournament—a tournament I was on the cusp of winning moments before Simon's outburst.

What I lack in literal football skills, I make up for in shuffling a small, triangular paper object across a flat surface. It was one of the only things that motivated me to go to school somedays. I had just scored a kickoff touchdown to put me in line for the win with a made extra point; everyone was bursting into cheers but were thankfully drowned out by the sound of wood shattering and swearing from the back of the room. Mr. Larson almost caught us mid-celebration—but thankfully he was more focused on turning back to the novel he was writing on the chalkboard.

It was hard to fault teachers like Mr. Larson for letting such destruction of property pass as nothing but a minor disturbance in their class. Before there were school psychologists dealing with delinquent behavior like Simon's, teachers were on their own. Given how grossly underpaid and underappreciated most teachers were, it was no wonder that someone like Simon could go relatively unchecked.

Our classmates nicknamed Simon as "Shorty," which stood for "short fuse," because any number of random things would cause Simon to become physically explosive. Like nicknaming a fat man, "Tiny," nicknaming Simon "Shorty" was equally funny and ironic; he was a six-foot five brickhouse, having been held back twice—the type of person who could pluck off pencil sharpeners that were bolted to the wall.

Simon's triggers were never the same thing. Unpredictable in the worst of ways, Simon was a loose cannon who instilled the fear of God into students and teachers alike. Most everybody gave him a wide berth, which I am sure wasn't helpful for Simon's already nonexistent self-esteem, but there were too many horror stories about kids who had been in the danger zone unknowingly. Unsurprisingly, Simon didn't have many friends.

Being kind to the likes of outcast behemoths like Simon provided mixed results for my social life. I initially didn't realize that striking up a conversation with Simon was such an unusual act. I was genuinely curious about who he was and why so many people feared for their lives when in his company. So, one day I asked him about his Incredible Hulk-like flareups and he told me. It turned out Simon had a condition called spontaneous explosiveness disorder, which was really difficult for his family and him to cope with. That information stuck with me enough to not avoid him like everybody else seemed to do.

It's not like I wanted to be best buds with him, but I really didn't mind that Simon thought of me as his friend. It's just that I was growing less excited about our relationship as time went on because of how often I was singled out as his sole friend, and therefore his only "caretaker." As awesome as I was at paper football, I think people thought of me as the quintessential "nice guy." This no doubt inspired teachers to constantly assign Simon to my groups. But our association was really becoming a drain on my ability to secure popularity points, especially with girls. I knew Simon wasn't as bad an apple as people thought, and that he was a good guy for 99% of the time, but that one percent of the time he *wasn't?* Unlike Yellowstone's Old Faithful or Adam Sandler's *Waterboy* character, not even Simon knew when he would erupt.

I couldn't blame others for being so afraid around him because the unpredictability of his disorder *was* terrifying. That said, I was also tired of people assuming I enjoyed being with him *all the time*. Maybe I was overly sensitive about it, but I swear a school day didn't go by without Shorty and Steve Harding being mentioned in the same sentence. If our association had been slightly more favorable, as in, if people thought I was a fearless badass or something, maybe hangin' with Shorty would've come with more benefits. After all, I *wasn't* afraid of him. I don't know why I wasn't afraid other than assuming it had to do with my good instincts, a strength that I was growing to appreciate and trust more and more—the kind of thing that helped me navigate when Shorty might go off. But those good instincts were also a nuisance. Sometimes I *hated* having such a kind conscience and finely tuned intuition. Being constantly assigned Shorty-duty had made me resentful, and I longed to be known for something different, something *better*.

Going into Mr. Larson's group assignment announcements, I'm sure most of my classmates assumed that Shorty would be assigned to my group. What they didn't know was that I had been anticipating this group project for months—and Shorty was not in my plans. You see, my older sister Jessica had taken this class a few years ago and said that Mr. Larson *never* changed. That meant that I could anticipate the same group project she and her classmates were assigned a couple years ago. From the beginning of the year, I *knew* what was coming down the line—so I plotted my steps carefully. Methodically. No one other than my two best friends knew that I was ready to shed being "Shorty's sidekick." I was eager to make a movie of my own, and I saw this as the perfect opportunity to create something so kickass that my classmates, particularly Samantha Reck, the hottest babe in my class, would have no choice but to line up for a slice of Steve-o pie.

To get there, I knew I needed to orchestrate a reason why it would be in Mr. Larson's best interests to put Simon with someone else—I couldn't get what I wanted with *him* in tow. No. Not this time. I wanted a group setting where I wasn't talking people down from high places or applying first aid when his condition got the worst of him. It was clear that asking my teachers to stop pairing us wasn't working—each request was denied. Requests to work with my friends were equally dismissed. It was evident that our teachers must have made some kind of pact to never allow Shorty out of my sight, nor to allow my two best friends and me to work together, so that I wouldn't be distracted from the stick of dynamite I was entrusted to supervise.

So, determined to finally receive the break I deserved in my favorite class, I devised a strategy. To start with, I went out of my way to become tight with Mr. Larson—I memorized what his hobbies were, his favorite books and movies, and other information he leaked about his personal life. And then, whenever I had a chance to talk with him one on one, I'd chat him up using all those tidbits. Developing some solid rapport with him was essential to make sure the plan worked. I figured he wouldn't be too suspicious because most of the adults I knew loved to talk about themselves whenever a kid showed the slightest bit of interest. Plus, well, I was a nice guy—teachers knew that I respected where the line was because I rarely, if ever, crossed it.

Secondly, I dropped hints that being buds with Simon was exhausting and that was affecting my schoolwork—which was true, but not *entirely* true. I was just very lazy when it came to applying myself where moviemaking wasn't a possibility… which was everything but Media Arts.

Finally, I told my two best friends to name each other as their first choice and that I was going to name someone else. And not just *anyone* else, but Samantha Reck—who would naturally fall in love with me once she realized how cool I was after seeing me ace this project and getting to know me. Because *of course* our project would be amazing with Samantha in it—nearly every great movie starred a bombshell leading lady. Sure, the other groups would have *girls*, but Samantha wasn't just any *girl*—she was a young *woman*. From her brunette hair to her voluptuous figure, she was a teenage *supermodel*, a younger version of Cindy Crawford, the hottest woman on the planet. Her eyes an endless sea of deep brown, and her smile? Just thinking about it gave me wood. Yes, Samantha was coming into her maturity now, and every guy could *see* that wondrous transformation in real time. None of our heads stayed stationary whenever Samantha walked by. I admittedly didn't know much about her personality yet, but it was only a matter of time before she and I would be swapping stories and getting to know each other… if I could somehow find a way to get her into my Media Arts group project. I had a good feeling my dreams had a legitimate chance of becoming reality.

The plan ended there. My group just *had* to be Dean and Glen plus Samantha… plus anybody *other* than Shorty. It was what I wished for on my birthday, and I believed wholeheartedly that when a person wished for such things, that those who fulfilled such a thing—God?—granted them. This project was, after all, the last group project of our middle school years—surely someone else could keep tabs on Shorty this one time. My plan was destined to work.

I was overdue for a massive success story. I had endured my teachers and parents telling me for years to be "more thoughtful," "think positively," and to "apply myself." Well, now I was being thoughtful and positively applying myself to *this*. I was going way above and beyond what most kids my age would dream of doing to get what *they* wanted. I was more committed to this than all the other assignments of my schooling *combined*. Heck, I was more dedicated to this than any paper football tournament. I pleaded silently with the wish granter that this one of mine would come true—and if not this one, then at least Mr. Larson finally missing the desk.

You see, all year long, when Mr. Larson wasn't writing on the chalkboard, he did this thing where he would gradually lean back and sit down on the edge of his desk. This doesn't sound miraculous, I realize, but you see, Mr. Larson was an enormous human. How his oversized butt was able to perch steadily on the tiniest corner of desk was baffling—it defied the laws of physics. I can't count how many times that seemingly insignificant event was the topic of our lunchroom conversations. We discussed interfering and greasing the desk so he would slip and fall off, but then the game would be over, and no one wanted that, especially since the fall wouldn't technically *count*. We wanted to see it happen *naturally*; so badly that any time he started to pace it was like an unspoken game—a collective yearning— had commenced, and not a single student wanted to miss *that one time* Mr. Larson's spatial awareness failed and he fell to the ground in an epic crash.

Mr. Larson had finally finished writing on the board and turned to face us. He began his usual pacing, and at this, the class grew deathly quiet and attentive, all thoughts of paper football forgotten. The energy in the room was palpable. Kids were sitting on the edge of their seats. You could feel the longing in our collective hearts, all beating a little more rapidly. *Was this the day? Were we about to witness history?* Mr. Larson, our heavyset, eighth grade Media Arts teacher, strode about the front, pants characteristically hanging by god-knows-what from his useless belt, as we watched, transfixed, like a cat behind the glass of a birdcage. And then, at the point of no return, he leaned backward ever so slightly, hand outstretched lackadaisically, as it probed for the corner of his desk—and as every student held their breath and leaned closer, his butt rested upon the smallest section of desk. And once again, Mr. Larson had inexplicably stuck the landing! The class sighed in disappointment.

"I know, fifty percent of your grade for one assignment might seem unfair for those of you on the fence, but think positively!"

Mr. Larson looked in our direction and smiled. Snapping out of my trance, his words registered.

"Fifty percent," I whispered under my breath to no one in particular.

"And now, without further ado, your group assignments!"

The electricity in the classroom had waned after Mr. Larson's odds-defying landing but returned instantly with the change of subject—it was time to learn *who* we'd be making our projects with.

"I've got a good feeling about this, Steve. I've been thinking positively all day!" Dean hissed in my ear from his desk behind me.

My best friend since we were three, Dean Peterson, who owned hand-me-down *Nike Jordans* from his older brother, had every right for optimism. I too had a good feeling about our chances—and when Dean and I both felt the same way about something, we were usually right.

I had Dean by an inch or two in height, but his olive skin, dark hair, and his ability to roll perfectly frayed jeans gave me plenty of reason to think my best friend had an inside track to graduating out of "dorkville" before me. I was so *average* compared to Dean. He was a gifted musician and could hold his own when it came to athletics, too. I wanted to measure up, especially with his mastery of *those jeans*—how did he do that?! That said, Dean didn't have the same feel for his instincts as I did, especially when it came to social intelligence and street smarts. That was something I preferred having an edge on, even if he was light years beyond me in his immaculate fashion sense.

"Class, I've divided you into four groups of five," Mr. Larson chuckled. "I've surprised myself this time, really outdone myself. Not all of you got your first choice, but some of you did—and I'm happy to report that one group is going to be very happy, because every single member received their first choice," he added, looking in our direction.

"We did it. It worked!" Glen said under his breath as he squeezed my elbow unusually hard.

Glen, my second closest friend, who constantly underestimated his brutish strength, released his squeeze after I yelped in pain.

I was growing hopeful the plan had indeed worked as I watched Mr. Larson walk around the room dividing students into groups. But there were still two groups left to be assigned and Shorty had not yet been named, meaning I had a fifty percent chance.

"Group three," Mr. Larson quipped as he walked over to our desks.

"The moment of truth," I whispered.

"Dean Peterson, Glen Hogan, Steve Harding, Samantha Reck, and Tom Edison, who will be the project leader."

Glen, Dean, and I exhaled and exchanged high fives and cheers. Glen pulled me close.

"Now don't blow your load, Harding, and keep your dick in your pants!" Glen fired. I blushed, then reached back and hit him as hard as I could.

I heard our names—plus Samantha's, and almost didn't register that the last group member wasn't Shorty. I looked over to see if he was as shocked as I had been, but he was still busily trying to reattach the pencil sharpener to the wall. If he cared, he didn't show it. In Shorty's place was Tom Edison. I realized he must have had the hots for Samantha and marked her as his first choice too. If so, this did not bode well for me. Tom Edison was a heartthrob, or so the girls constantly gushed to every boy not named Tom Edison.

"Each group has two weeks to complete the project. I've assigned a leader for each group, and this person is responsible for the camcorder, settling any disputes as needed, and other leadership duties. Please go to the media center to check out your school-issued camcorder, which will have a blank tape preloaded. Be careful, these are not toys and we don't have replacements. You will be graded on historical accuracy, creativity, group participation, and video length. Keep it under five minutes if you can, but certainly no longer than eight minutes. Stick to the subject you're assigned—no trading!"

The room erupted as students immediately began moving around and finding their groupmates. I turned to face Dean as Glen moved his desk closer. Samantha was nowhere to be seen, presumably out of the classroom for her individual band lesson time, and Tom, *not Shorty*—something that I was still trying to believe—began making his way from the other end of the classroom.

"We did pray for *anybody* but Shorty, but him? Oh well," Glen said.

"Honestly, who names their kid *Tom Edison*?" Dean hissed as he glared at Tom, who was standing next to Mr. Larson's desk with the other group leaders.

It was a popular dig Dean used regarding our classmate Tom. The question fell on deaf ears however, for that's about all Dean ever said about him. Belittling his name was the only jab he had because so little else was known about Tom. We could only speculate about him and his backstory because he kept so much to himself, and no one in school really seemed to know anything about him. Which was too bad because I would've loved to have someone like Tom in my corner.

He was polite, didn't bully anyone, and he was extremely popular with the girls due to his wavy blond hair, bright smile, and flawless complexion. He was a straight A student, tall, fit, and tremendously athletic; Tom appeared to have it all. He was usually first pick for basketball and other sports in gym.

Teachers adored him, too—he was always asking and answering teacher's questions, which stroked their egos. And yet, Tom was a lone wolf. He didn't appear to have any friends and didn't belong to any organized clubs or teams. He turned down invitations to meet up with girls or to go to the parties thrown by the popular kids. Tom wasn't a jerk to anyone, but he never seemed interested in befriending anyone either. As I began to ponder again who Tom's first choice for this group project was, he pulled up a chair, spun it around, and straddled it backwards.

"H–hey T–Tom, h–how's it going?" Glen asked, as if afraid of him.

"Good! You-guys-have-any-big-plans-this-weekend-want-to-sleepover-at-my-house-tonight-so-we-can-start-planning-our-group-project?"

I was lost for words. Neither Dean, Glen, nor I said one word for what felt like thirty seconds. We just stared at him, dumbfounded. Unphased, Tom smiled and strummed his fingers on the back of the seat he was sitting on.

Here was this guy who had rarely spoken to any of us all year, and was now asking if *me* and *my friends* could sleep over at *his* house? I looked at Dean and Glen and tried to see what they were thinking, and they were looking just as I was feeling. The silence was deafening. We needed to say *something*.

"Yeah, dude, that'd be cool," Glen spoke up and saved the awkward silence from getting too out of hand.

"Uh, yeah, but uh, I can't tonight—it's Shabbat at sundown," Dean said, barely audible.

"Are your grandparents in town again, or what?" I asked.

"Yup," Dean replied.

Dean's parents were notoriously lax when it came to practicing their faith, but whenever his mom's supremely devout parents came for a visit, suddenly Dean's mom and dad were also supremely devout. I'm sure Dean's insides were churning having to speak up and out his religiosity like that, even though most of us were aware Dean was in fact, Jewish. Talking about religion just wasn't something most of our classmates seemed to do, and most of them were from Christian families besides, so it made it even more uncomfortable for Dean to talk about in front of people.

"That's ok, we don't have to," Tom said.

First, he goes for it and now he was dropping the sleepover invitation *altogether*? Why was he giving up so fast? My instincts were telling me this was odd.

"Well, why not Saturday night?" I chimed.

Dean and Glen exchanged glances. It wasn't the first time Dean's grandparents came to town, so I knew that by sundown *Saturday*, Dean would be free. I'd have to skip going to my own church that Sunday morning, but I figured my mom would insist I accepted Tom's offer. In fact, she would probably be *thrilled* at my opportunity to glimpse behind the Edison family curtain. I laughed to myself, knowing how excited my mom, the neighborhood gossip queen, would be to have *her son* have the inside track on someone like Tom, whose parents were every bit as mysterious to other adults as Tom was to his classmates.

"Great! Here's my address. How about tomorrow then, at seven o'clock? Should we invite Samantha for a few hours?"

"Hell yes we should," said Glen, nodding at me.

"I'll ask her!" I almost yelled, surprising myself as Dean's eyes bugged out and Glen smiled. Tom scribbled his address on a piece of paper and handed it to me. I copied it down on another piece of paper and stared at it, the reality of what I'd just volunteered for dawning on me with mixed horror and exhilaration.

***

I decided to wait until only a few minutes were left in between classes to make my approach. That way, if things went poorly, which seemed to me a high probability, I could make my escape look less obvious as students emptied from the hallways and into classrooms.

Samantha had her beautiful backside to me, fumbling with something in her locker as I did my best to walk with confidence toward her.

"Hey Samantha?" I asked.

She turned around and I swear time slowed down as she did; hair sweeping across those bottomless brown eyes, a smile forming on those plush lips that every guy in school would slice their left pinky off for a chance to kiss.

"Oh, hi Steve! What's up?"

"Hi," I said, forgetting who I was.

"Hi," she laughed, looking side to side.

"Uh, yeah. So, Mr. Larson—"

"Did he fall off the desk?!"

I laughed more than I should have. Samantha just stared at me, almost glaring—but I think that had more to do with the fact that she thought she had missed the historic moment.

"No, no. I—no. He somehow landed again. I don't know how, but—"

"Oh my god, I thought for sure he fell. I was about to give up playing bassoon forever so I wouldn't be reminded that I missed the big mo—"

"Ha, no, he very much did not fall on his ass in class," I said, instantly regretting the rhyme, certain she thought less of me for it. I pushed through my self-doubt before what little courage I had left imploded. "Mr. Larson assigned the final project groups, and you were assigned to my—our—group," I concluded.

"Cool! Who else is in our group?"

"Glen, Dean, and Tom…Edison," I said.

Why had I felt the need to add Tom's last

name? There weren't any other Tom's in Media Arts class, nor even in our grade. His full name was seared into my brain, it was almost impossible separating the two—the opposite of a celebrity name like Madonna, which stood on its own. It was weird. If my instincts were right, and Samantha had chosen him and not me as her first choice, then maybe I was subconsciously doing everything I could to sabotage my competition.

"Whoa! That's awesome! I can't believe I'm in a group with—"

At that exact moment, Samantha's two closest friends appeared out of thin air, the backs of their jean jackets slamming into the lockers beside us, Tootsie Pops dancing across their lips.

"Hey, Steve," Brittany said, her voice dripping with superiority.

"Where's your friend, *the 'tard?*" spat her devious twin sister, Belinda.

Every part of my body clenched when she uttered the slur, and the erection that I had been doing my best to keep at bay instantly disappeared. I was taught from a young age that boys were never, ever, allowed to hit a girl, but I was certain that insulting people for having a condition like Simon's was grounds for rule infractions like that one.

"Ugh! You are the worst! Quit calling people that!" Samantha roared as she slammed her locker closed.

Brittany and Belinda shared a wicked smile.

"Oh Samantha, don't be such a prude," Brittany said.

Samantha rolled her eyes and started to walk away. I instinctively walked with her, even though my class was in the opposite direction.

"You and 'everybody's friend' a thing now or what?" Belinda called after us.

Belinda's first put-down had made me want to smack that Tootsie Pop off her face. And now she'd shouted out my detested nickname and exposed my ultimate fantasy about Samantha. It sent me over the edge—I wanted to kill her and find a way to make it look like an accident.

Steve 'everybody's friend' Harding—that's what some of my classmates called me behind my back. Those two words 'everybody's friend' taken together should be flattering, but I grew to hate the title. It was the inevitable consequence of being nice to Shorty, and other "loser" kids like him. But even though I hated that being nice to people made me uncool, I resented even more the fact that being mean to others was often what it took to be considered popular. Belinda and her twin Brittany were like a two-headed dragon, and if there was anything about Samantha that I didn't understand, it was why she was friends with those monsters.

Brittany and Belinda were almost as attractive as Samantha. Puberty had clearly visited the Bowers twins before anyone else—and the *girls* clearly knew it, too. They would stick their breasts out everywhere they went, causing guys to trip over themselves or run into open doors and trash cans. Even in the dead of winter they'd wear something that revealed their extra flesh. They seemed to think those things were Olympic gold medals draped around their necks. None of us knew what to do with such displays of cleavage. I imagined it was like a driver's eyes being pulled to the side of the road, gawking at an overturned car in the ditch. I half-wondered if they got a pass for being so cruel because so few ever actually heard anything they said. Their boobs were not enough to quell my distaste for them—I'd rather lick the bottom side of a toilet seat than spend five minutes in the same room. How Samantha could spend so much time with them was beyond me. She had stood up for Simon *this* time, but who knows if she would've done the same if I hadn't been standing there.

I knew there were far worse nicknames a guy could have, but if shedding the nice guy label was what it was going to take to go out with someone like Samantha, then it wasn't going to be easy. I really wanted Samantha to see me as someone she could be more than friends with, but I didn't see why it was so fun making others feel miserable. Brittany, Belinda, and their other friends were no doubt the most popular in our class, but they were also the meanest, and I wasn't sure how I felt about joining their ranks if Samantha and I became—well, *a thing*.

We walked side by side in silence until she got

to the door of her next class.

"The guys and I are sleeping over at Tom's tomorrow night. Want to come over for the first part so we can start planning?"

I handed her Tom's address before she answered. She looked at me with those to-die-for brown eyes and flashed me that man-eating smile. Sweat accumulated on my scalp and my groin came back to life. *I need to get the hell out of here.*

"See you tomorrow night, Samantha," I said and then quickly turned around and sprinted toward my classroom at the far end of the hallway, probably looking like a total jackass.

***

As suspected, my mom was *ecstatic* about Tom's sleepover invitation. She wouldn't shut up about it, blabbering my dad's ear off about it over supper Saturday night. Since my mom volunteered to drive the three of us, I ate as fast as I could before running upstairs to get my things from my room. On the way to my bedroom, I passed my sister's door, which was barely muffling what sounded like my favorite band, Metallica, on the other side of it. *I thought Jessica told me she hated my music. This is just weird.* I planted my ear to her door. Jessica was talking while the music blared—not *singing* along but *talking.* I wondered if she had a guy in there, so I tested the doorknob and found it unlocked. I took a deep breath before I burst into her room, ready to catch her in the act of having an illegal guest.

"Ah–ha! Busted!" I yelled as I whipped open the door.

Jessica had her back to me and didn't even flinch. "Enter Sandman," from the self-titled *Metallica* album, drowned out my sudden appearance. I stood in the doorway and studied the scene. There was a stack of CDs on her desk as well as several individual sheets of paper placed neatly side by side. She was speaking dramatically to herself. She wasn't on the phone and no one else was in the room with her besides me. Of *course,* I thought, *She's rehearsing her lines for her play. But why in the world is she wasting the excellence of Metallica like this?* She remained completely unaware of my presence.

Ahh, but now I had a rare opportunity to scare the daylights out of my sister; a justifiable act because she had not only stolen my Metallica album, but she wasn't even listening to it! I tip-toe'd closer. When I was within reach, I yelled, "Jessica!"

I ducked just before her fist slammed into my face. I was simultaneously awed by her haymaker— and enraged.

"What the hell, Jessica?" I spat as I picked myself off the floor.

She shut the music off and glared at me.

"I was running my lines, you little shit. Don't you know how to knock?"

"I tried, but—"

"Really?" she asked, her tone shifting from rage to curiosity.

"Yeah, well—I didn't exactly *knock*, but – but I opened the door and yelled. I thought you were in here with a dude," I said.

"Ha! It works!"

I stared at her. She continued.

"I borrowed your terrible music so I could practice my lines—I'm trying to perfect my stage presence so that nothing fazes me," she said.

"Borrow? No, no, no. That's called *robbery*," I shot back.

I spotted more of my music on her desk— Nirvana *Nevermind*, Guns N' Roses *Appetite for Destruction*, and my *Master of Puppets* Metallica album, too. I had painstakingly saved up money from mowing the lawn to purchase each one of these CDs from Columbia House, and I wasn't about to let my sister get away with treating them like anything less than the treasures they were. Getting those packages delivered in the mail were the *best* days.

"I left a note, didn't you see it?"

"No, Jessica, I did not. I was on my way to my room to grab my stuff for tonight's sleepover at Tom Edison's house."

"Oh really? What on earth are you hanging out with him for?"

"None of your business," I said.

"Who else is going to be there?"

"I said *none of your business*."

She stepped threateningly toward me. I stood my ground.

"Dean and Glen, and—you know what, never mind. I gotta go. Give back my CDs and steal someone else's music, will ya?"

She crossed her arms and looked at her stolen goods stacked in a column upon her immaculate desk.

"But I've just had a *breakthrough*, Steve! C'mon, let me use them! This can really set me apart!" she pled.

"What's in it for me?" I fired back.

Jessica thought for a moment.

"Girl advice," she quipped as she raised her eyebrows.

"Pfft, I don't need any of that," I replied, although my shaky voice and reddening cheeks likely gave me away.

"I remember 8th grade, Steve. Final offer," she said and uncrossed her arms and extended her hand.

"Fine," I said and shook it.

"Thanks bro. Have fun at the sleepover. And tell that pervert Glen to stop taping his love letters to my locker or I might turn them in as evidence for stalking."

***

My mom was unusually quiet during the trip, no doubt casing the neighborhood where Tom lived and rehearsing her introduction to Tom's parents.

Tom's house was an unassuming split level in a new housing development at the edge of town. There were few neighbors, and the house clearly looked custom built. There wasn't much to the front yard, but the backyard was massive, and there was a heavily wooded area nearby. Tom and his parents were eagerly awaiting us on the driveway in front of their two-car garage. Tom's parents and my mom made some small chat while Dean, Glen, and I bolted for the basement, where Tom's bedroom was. Tom was the basement's sole occupant. I didn't spot a television, but instead saw a massive train set-type construction in the center of the room.

"What in the world is—" I asked.

"That's my dad's. He's kind of a dork about the Bible. It's a model of ancient Jerusalem and the countryside where various Bible stories come from. He's built all this himself and needed a basement large enough so he could store it," he said, almost apologetically.

We walked around it in silence, taking it all in. I noticed a tripod and a top-of-the-line Sony camcorder tilting down toward the model. Tom must have been watching me because he anticipated my next question.

"He's also a filmmaking nut. He likes to record these tiny figures using stop-motion animation that this camcorder captures well. His office upstairs has the only TV in the house so he can edit and watch his movies when he's finished making them."

The doorbell rang. Samantha had arrived. Tom ascended the steps, leaving the three of us on our own.

"Jesus, this dude is even weirder than we thought!" Glen said.

"I know!" Dean said.

"Look, this is our last hurrah before high school, and I'm not letting Tom ruin our fun. Plus, Samantha is in our group! *Samantha*!" I hissed and pointed upstairs, color forming in my cheeks as I tried to absorb all the new information about Tom's family… all while my blood rushed out of my brain and into my loins at the promise of Samantha's arrival. "So let's go out with a bang."

"I don't think Samantha is that kind of gal, Steve-o," Glen said. We burst into hysterical laughter, falling to the ground in tears as Tom and Samantha made their way down the steps.

"Oh boy, what did I miss?" Tom asked as he and Samantha watched us rolling on the ground trying to regain our composure.

"Nothing!" Dean and I yelled in unison. I shot Glen a look that telepathically begged for his silence. We busted out laughing again.

***

The five of us reclined on the floor of Tom's basement, plotting. The smell of Samantha's perfume was intoxicating. It took every ounce of inner strength to not look at her the entire time. We didn't have a natural conversation starter with Tom in our midst; typically, we'd probably debate whether he was in the witness protection program or if he was an alien, but with him there we were forced to talk about other things. It would have made sense to use our time together more productively—like by asking Tom about himself so we wouldn't have to guess anymore, or by actually working on our project. Instead, we talked about everybody else who wasn't there: teachers, neighbors, classmates, the clerk at the grocery store, even the guy who tried to budge in front of Glen at *Old Country Buffet*.

It wasn't surprising that we used the two hours with Samantha to discuss virtually *nothing* about our assignment. What *was* surprising was how flirtatious *Dean* was with the love of *my* life. I had done everything in my power to be cool, to act normal, to not actively try to get Samantha to fall in love with me—but that was clearly not the strategy of my best friend. No, he had a different agenda coming into this meeting, and I wasn't the only one who noticed. After Samantha left and the sleepover portion of the evening commenced, the gloves came off in a hurry.

"What the *hell* was that, Dean? Did you *actually* think you would get away with complimenting the smell of her hair without us tearing you apart for it?" I asked, incredulous.

"Uh, that obvious huh?"

"Obvious? No, no. The *obvious* flirting was laughing *hysterically* at every attempt at humor she made. But complimenting her hair? That was suave, brother, *suave*," Glen joked.

"Sorry, guys. I just need to step up my game, that's all."

"Game? What game? You have no game," I added.

"Exactly. And my brother has been a real *asshole* about it. He keeps calling me a queer. Thinks it's weird that I don't have a girlfriend and *gay* how often I hang out with you guys."

"Your *brother* said that? That's – that's pretty fucked up," Tom whispered, almost to himself.

Our heads whipped around to look at him, jaws dropped at Tom's first f-bomb in our presence.

"I–I just… I mean, I don't have any brothers and I… I mean, that's a *rotten* thing to call someone without knowing i–if a person was… and I guess, well, I mean, why would your own brother…." Tom stumbled on his words. It was the first time I'd seen him lose his composure like that. His face flushed bright red as he fell silent and diverted his eyes. It was weird. Then I remembered how horrified I was the first time I met Dean's brother—even when we were little kids, he tormented us. And so, I resented Jacob even more for somehow managing to offend Tom, too. Dean's brother was the epitome of a douchebag and had a way of making everyone feel terrible, even when he wasn't physically in the room.

"Well, I'm *not* gay—I'm just not great with the ladies, that's all," Dean said.

Silence followed. At that time in our pubescent male lives, there wasn't anything much worse than being labeled queer. When a guy said those words to another guy, he was questioning his masculinity. Being accused of homosexuality was the next level up from saying you acted like a girl. It was about weakness. I don't think any of us knew anything about feminism or gay rights at that time of our lives; we just knew that someone calling you a girl, or a *fag* required you to defend your honor by showcasing your toughness and by being a ladies' man.

Dean and I shared siblings of the same age: my older sister, Jessica, and Dean's brother Jacob. Jessica and I mostly kept to ourselves, especially when Dean and Glen were over—but that had to do with Glen's immense crush on my sister, not because we disliked one another. I was sure Dean thought of Jessica like an older sister, given how long our families had known each other; but that wasn't the case for me with Dean's older brother, Jacob. He was nothing less than a bully. Jessica at least tolerated us; even on Glen's most persistent days, Jessica took the high road instead of fighting back or belittling us. There were even moments when I think she genuinely enjoyed our company. Jacob, on the other hand, was not someone to be trusted. We knew from a young age to always keep our guard up around him.

If there was anyone more detestable than Brittany and Belinda Bowers, it was Jacob Peterson.

Jacob made it very evident that he resented us. We avoided him at all costs because otherwise he made us pay, either by physical or verbal abuse. He and his friends delighted in bullying Dean and me every chance they had. The only time we were safe was when Glen was around. It never ceased to amaze me how Glen's presence deterred interference and bullying; it was a combination of Glen's lack of filter, self-assurance, and grown man's physical strength— not to mention his oversized gut. Even Jacob would be surprisingly avoidant around him. As much as we all wanted not to care about Jacob's opinion of us, he was a high school standout who always dated the prettiest girls, so what he thought about us mattered. Still, his treatment of Dean his entire life really rankled me, and I'd always dreamed of getting back at him for it someday.

Jessica, on the other hand, was equally popular, but for different reasons. Like Jacob, Jessica was a standout athlete and student. She displayed little interest in the dating scene, but she told my parents that had more to do with her classmates' lack of maturity than anything else. What intimidation and bullying were to Jacob, unbridled joy and kindness were to Jessica. She was fun-loving and genuine in an innocent way. Jessica and I weren't besties by any means, but I knew she would have my back and would help me if I ever needed her.

With Jacob, it was much, much different. Dean preferred to be invisible around him. That Jacob had said such an insult to him was maybe not a shocking development, but very disturbing, and no doubt a motivating factor for Dean to step up his game around the female gender—even obnoxiously flirting with Samantha. I forgave his behavior and was eager to move on.

"He is such a prick. Wish he'd just mind his own damn business. Forget about him, Dean," Glen said.

"Yeah. Easy for you to say, but yeah. I know."

After consoling Dean with a couple of pats on the back, he perked up and provided a much-desired change of subject.

"So, I was thinking about our movie, and I think we should make it into a spy thriller—like a James Bond kind of thing. We can try to find a way to include Glen's new paintball gun," Dean said excitedly.

"Definitely. I just bought a new box of ammo. We have enough rounds to obliterate the Third Reich," Glen gushed.

"I knew it was going to be fun to work with you guys," Tom said. "But I haven't exactly seen a lot of good movies. I've only been allowed to watch PG and G ones."

"Oh, come on, you've never snuck into your dad's office and binged a bunch of rated R movies?" Glen asked.

Tom shook his head.

"No way. His office is strictly off limits. I'd

get into so much trouble if I got caught doing that kind of thing."

"You have this entire basement to yourself, and your parents don't let you have a TV?"

"No—they're not like most parents, I guess," Tom said quietly.

What kind of parents didn't allow their kid to watch TV? The thought that we were spending the night at someone's house and wouldn't have the ability to watch a movie during the wee hours was completely foreign to Dean and me—that's all we'd done for most of our friendship. The arrival of Glen two years ago pushed us out of the house more, but even Glen enjoyed movie-marathoning almost every weekend. We have collectively seen a thousand movies, easily. The three of us came to the realization of our strange night to-be at the same time and sat there in total silence.

"So, you've never seen *any* movies about war or guns or anything cool? *Star Wars*? *Indiana Jones*? *James Bond*?" I asked.

"Not yet," Tom said, growing red in the face.

Tom's statement felt like someone shattering a plate glass window with a brick. How could someone make it to eighth grade and have never seen *Star Wars*?!

"My mom is stricter about it than my dad. He's starting to ease up a little. So, I've seen a few of the classics, but that's about it," Tom added.

"How many is a few?" Dean asked.

"I don't know, maybe like—ten?"

"Ten?!"

"Keep your voices down!" Tom loudly whispered as he looked above him.

A few moments later, the basement door opened and Mr. Edison started to come down the stairs.

"Tom, your voices are getting a little loud. Your mother and I will be going to bed shortly," said Mr. Edison in the calmest scolding tone I'd ever heard.

Mr. Edison wore a red flannel robe, which was exactly what you'd expect someone sporting such a perfectly manicured Tom Selleck mustache to wear. He was built like Selleck, too, and that Magnum P.I. physique made me both nervous and jealous—Tom's dad could have very well been an international spy with guns like those biceps. I didn't know what I expected Tom's parents to look like, but after comparing Tom to his dad, it made sense; heartthrobs share DNA.

"Sure Dad, no sweat. Sorry 'bout that," Tom said politely.

"Thanks buddy. Say, Tom? Have you mentioned to your friends about tomorrow morning?"

Tom's eyes ballooned. We stared at Tom but said nothing. His dad then mouthed the word "church" at him.

"No, not yet. I will. You can go to bed now, ok? Sorry about the yelling."

Just when it felt like we were in the clear, Mr. Edison turned his attention to us.

"How rude of me, I don't believe Tom gave us a chance to introduce ourselves; you boys hustled down here so quickly when you arrived. I suppose you were excited to start your big project. How *exciting*. Oh, hang on – Shelly?—" he looked up the stairs.

"It's cool, we can meet her tomorrow," Tom interjected, an air of ominous dread in his voice.

"Nonsense, she's right here! Honey? Do you have a second? I'd like for you to meet Tom's classmates!"

Another pause. Then more footsteps coming down the stairs. And then Mrs. Edison appeared, wearing a full-blown pink nightgown with curlers in her hair.

"Oh hello! So good to meet you! Welcome to our home! It is *so* good to see Tom making *new friends*. I'm so happy that you boys could come over tonight."

Tom looked like he was going to pass out. His face was the color of his dad's red flannel robe.

"Ahh. Yep. Good to meet you, too," Glen chirped.

"Well, we will let you boys get back to…."

"Our movie," Tom whispered.

"Ahh yes, your *movie*. Excellent. We're excited to hear *all about* it. Have fun boys. But don't stay up all night! We don't want you sleeping in and missing church!" Mrs. Edison squealed.

More silence. It was so embarrassing—like hearing an adult talk about sex for the first time. How does one speak after *that* conversation? Everything was so fundamentally horrible and hilarious at the same time. Our mouths were hanging wide open. Tom was slumped over, his hands over his face, not breathing. Glen, Dean, and I continued to look up at the stairs, trying to evaluate what had transpired. Glen broke the silence.

"So, which *ten* movies?"

Dean and I exchanged smiles. Glen leaned closer to Tom, looking for a sign of movement. Suddenly, Tom's shoulders started shaking. As if things couldn't get *more* awkward and uncomfortable! Now he was *bawling* his eyes out right in front of us. We continued to exchange incredulous looks, paralyzed and unable to comprehend what was happening. I began formulating an escape plan. But Tom wasn't crying, he was *laughing*! And then, in one enormous swoop, Tom's body flung backwards and let loose uncontrollable cackling. Soon the four of us were sprawled on the ground laughing, too. This went on for a couple minutes until we heard footsteps at the stairway door open again.

"Boys? Your mother and I really need to get some sleep. Please. Keep. It. Down."

All Tom could manage was a stifled mutter that sounded like, "Mmmf." Whatever it was, it worked, and the door closed.

"I am *so* sorry about that, guys," Tom said apologetically, trying to get past the giggles.

"Sorry about *what*? I'm still trying to figure out exactly *what* happened," I said.

"And I don't mean to sound rude, but… we're not really expected to get up tomorrow and go to *church,* are we?" Dean asked.

Suddenly Tom looked around, as if trying to make sure there was no one else listening.

"Well, here's the thing—"

We leaned closer.

"—my parents have this thing about *church.* We cannot miss a Sunday. So, just because *you're* here, doesn't mean *I* get a pass. And neither do *you* guys."

"But—" I began. I was really looking forward to staying up all night and sleeping in, which required having no obligations in the morning—especially not something I'd have to be coherent for.

"Yeah, fine, whatever. We'll make it work. Might be kind of fun," Dean said.

"Ok, cool. Thanks. I promise to make it as easy as possible on you."

A few moments of silence followed, but before it got out of hand again, Tom wisely changed the subject.

"Mr. Larson assigned us World War Two for our video subject. Should we have Samantha play Anne Frank, or do you guys have something else in mind?" Tom asked.

Dean, Glen, and I exchanged incredulous looks. Startled, Tom looked at us with almost as much incredulity.

"We can't have *Samantha Reck* play Anne Frank. That's lame. Samantha is a *fox*, dude. The hottest girl in our class—and probably a top five babe in the whole school, even including Steve's sister, Jessica *Hard-on*," Glen said.

"Shut up, Glen!" I yelled.

I punched him in the arm. Glen broke into laughter and started his typical elaborations about my sister and his plans to sweep her off her feet, marry her, and have a house full of kids together someday.

"Let's come up with something else, maybe like an alternate ending to the Nazi regime or something," I suggested while trying to shush Glen's fantasizing.

***

"Tom?! Time to eat breakfast!" Tom's mom shouted from the door at the top of the-stairs.

Glen, Dean, and I awoke with a start, but Tom was still sound asleep.

"Tom?! It's seven o'clock! Your breakfast is getting cold!" his mom yelled again.

The three of us looked at each other in disbelief. We had never gotten up this early after staying up most of the night. But Tom was *still* asleep.

"Tom?" his mom yelled *again* from the top of

the basement steps.

"*Jesus Christ, we're up!*" I yelled without thinking.

Glen and Dean glared at me. I shrugged. Mrs. Edison closed the door. I wasn't used to that kind of rude awakening. Glen shook Tom awake and we stared at him until he grew uncomfortable. He didn't seem to mind that he'd slept through the wake-up call from his way-too-perky mom. We got dressed and made our way upstairs for breakfast.

"Tom? Can I speak with you for a second?"

"Sure, Mom," Tom said going over to her.

Mrs. Edison put her arm around her son as the two walked away from the kitchen. Just before disappearing around a corner, Tom's mom tossed the three of us an icy glare that made my skin crawl. My jaw loosened as I stared at the now empty spot where they'd just been. I was zoned out, wondering what we'd done to make her look at us like that that, when suddenly I was gagging because Glen had shoved a sausage into my gaping mouth. I coughed loudly, choking, but got the sausage down just as Tom and Mrs. Edison reappeared.

Glen whispered something to Dean, causing orange juice to erupt from Dean's nostrils. As Dean and Glen cackled silently to themselves, I gazed at the mouthwatering stack of pancakes and plate full of sausages, suddenly forgetting how tired I was. My stomach pushed aside the lingering annoyance about our early wake-up call and Mrs. Edison's disapproving look. I did my best to smile at Mrs. Edison, who was back to her exceptionally perky self. I fiercely resisted the urge to roll my eyes as her sing-song voice repeated, "This is the day," as she sipped from her coffee mug. I wondered if she took her coffee with cream or cocaine.

"Eat quickly boys, we need to leave in thirty-five minutes."

"I thought we were just going to church, Mom?" Tom asked.

"Oh, Thomas. Your Christian education is a priority, too," Mrs. Edison replied.

Tom gave his mom a fake smile and then shrank down in his chair. The rest of us looked at each other and then at Tom, who gazed back at us and grew very red in the face.

"It'll go fast," Tom whispered to us. "Just pretend you're *spies*."

"What?" we whispered back.

"You know, for our *movie*. Pretend you're undercover spies and my church is your mission location," Tom continued energetically.

"What are you boys talking about over there?" Mrs. Edison asked.

"Oh, nothing much. Just ideas for our movie," Tom said nonchalantly.

"You boys..." she said, shaking her head.

We hustled downstairs, grabbed our stuff, and talked over our plans for the morning. I wasn't as apprehensive about going to Tom's church anymore.

In fact, I was looking forward to it.

***

Tom's church was a massive building; it felt like walking into the entrance of a mall. I expected to see a movie theater and a food court inside. Dean and Glen elbowed me as Tom turned down a long hallway with several classrooms, one right after the other, just like at our school. We could faintly hear Mrs. Edison yell, "Have a great morning, Tom! I'll meet you by the sanctuary doors! I love you!"

We followed Tom through the church that was bustling with kids and adults, each adult who greeted us more chipper than the last one. They must have put the same "cream" in their coffee that Mrs. Edison did.

"Does this place have a confessional booth? I've always wanted to go into one of those and rip a juicy one," Glen said, looking around.

"It's not that kind of church, dumbass," I said.

"You better watch that potty mouth, Steve. We're in *God's house*," Glen shot back.

"Keep it down! We're supposed to be *spies* remember. Check your cover," said Dean.

"Exactly—you guys are on thin ice with my mom as it is," Tom said, causing us to come to a full stop, looking around fearfully.

"What? Why?" we asked in unison.

"Did you *swear* at my mom this morning?" Tom asked the three of us.

"No! Of course not!" we spat.

"She said one of you used the Lord's name in vain—and that 'that kind of behavior is unacceptable.'"

Dean and Glen turned their heads and looked at me.

"Oh Christ—*shit*! I mean, yeah—I did yell at her, sorry. I was just waking up and it just sort of spilled out," I confessed.

"Dude, she was *not* happy. You guys will need to redeem yourselves if you ever want to hang out again," Tom said, the latter half of the sentence lowering an octave or two.

"What do you suggest?" I asked.

"I don't know, just – just try not to stand out for the wrong reasons, okay?"

"Are there *right reasons* to stand out?" Dean asked.

Tom was deep in thought for a moment. Then he started to smile and looked us all in the eyes and spoke determinedly.

"Yeah, you know, there are. You can pay attention or like, *get involved*. My mom and other adults *love it* when I ask and answer questions and show that I care about stuff," Tom said.

Dean, Glen, and I looked at each other, dumbfounded but curious. Sensing our open-mindedness, Tom continued.

"I mean, my mom thinks you guys are *heathens* at this point. If you can, you know, just avoid breaking any of the Ten Commandments in her presence from now on, she'll probably come around," Tom concluded hopefully.

The four of us shared a laugh and continued walking. Glen continued to eye the room, probably looking for a place to fart.

"Well, what *are* we getting into?" I repeated.

"Uh… well, it's not like *school*. At Christian Ed you're going to have to be… *convincing*," Tom said in a hushed voice.

As we entered the classroom, about twenty kids turned and openly stared at us as if we were aliens or something. Tom walked right in and grabbed a few chairs without even noticing the other kids' glares. I pretended that I wasn't intimidated, but I was.

It wasn't just the number of kids, but the number of kids I didn't know. There were about twenty kids in my church's confirmation class, too. But they were kids I had known a long time, which made hiding and avoidance so much easier. Here I felt exposed and vulnerable. The idea of standing out as someone with knowledge or a strong interest in anything was deplorable—the last thing I wanted to worry about was adults having high expectations of me. But the truth was that I didn't mind thinking about religious things. Unlike Dean, who only had to care when his grandparents were in town, or Glen, whose parents didn't appear to believe in any higher power, I *did* possess knowledge and curiosity about

God and the Bible—and apparently so did Tom.

At my church, I may have been hiding behind everyone else, but that didn't keep me from listening and attaining information; I just never let that fascination or understanding show—not to Dean, to Glen, or to anyone. Tom's encouragement to get involved and to stand out for the right reasons sparked something within me; something about the way he said those things rang true. So, even though I felt nervous about the stares of forty or so eyeballs on us, my adrenaline was kicking in and I sensed that I had a rare opportunity to be someone different in a classroom setting. In Tom's class I didn't have my reputation to protect because I was a stranger here. There was a freedom in being unknown—I could experiment without much risk.

The teacher spotted the four of us and broke into a huge smile. I expected Glen to let one loose at any moment and ruin everyone's breakfast. When no sound or smell came, we followed Tom's lead, sitting and bowing our heads in silence. After the longest minute of my life, the teacher eliminated any chance of dozing off by launching into a rambling prayer… or was it a lecture? I was able to keep up for a while, and some of the things she said were really interesting. But she just kept going and I lost focus, especially with her use of at least twenty different names and adjectives about God.

Everyone said the "Amen" in unison. I kept my head bowed and eyes closed, lost in deep thought about how people at my church said the "Amen" with a short "a" and people here said it with a long "ahh." *Why do our two churches say it differently? Which is the right way? How do they say it in movies? How did the priest in* The Exorcist *say it?* This then led me to imagining one of the kids in the room becoming possessed and throwing chairs around. When I opened my eyes again, I was clearly the only one still "in prayer." Dean and Glen were laughing hysterically in my direction. I brushed concern for them aside and listened to what the teacher was saying.

"If prayer is our way of talking to God, what is *God's* way of talking to us?" she asked the class.

My thoughts rushed back to the little blond girl spewing vulgarity at the priest as he tried to silence the demon within her. Then out of nowhere I answered her question and said, "Through the preacher." This elicited another ear-to-ear smile from the teacher. Everyone's heads whipped toward me. Tom was smiling almost as much as the teacher. As if not wanting to be shown up by the new guy, the class started yelling their responses:

"Through the choir!" said a girl from the back.

"Through our *teachers*," said a brown-noser in the front row.

"Music!" said a boy right next to me.

"Nature!" said a girl who was looking out the window.

"Friends!" said Tom with a huge smile.

"Parents!" said Glen with an equally large

smile, mischievous as ever.

"Bratwurst!" said someone from behind us in a squeaky voice.

The class burst into laughter. We looked to see who had yelled "bratwurst." The culprit sat in the furthest back corner of the room. He was a chubby short kid, grinning widely.

"Marty, would you be so kind as to elaborate on your answer?"

"Um, no. You really *don't want to know*," he replied with a grin.

Everyone laughed. The teacher calmed everyone down and continued, asking if there were any other ways that people could receive direction from God. I glanced over at Tom, and I could tell that he knew something but was not in any hurry to share it. Then I noticed the teacher was staring at him, too. She seemed to be waiting for Tom to make eye contact with her. Running out of patience, she asked aloud, "What do *you* think, Tom?"

"The Bible," Tom replied at once.

"Exactly. God loves to speak to us through the *Bible*. The Bible is God's way of telling the world about him and his love through *Jesus*."

For reasons I'm still unsure of, I yelled, "Amen" (with a long sounding "a"). Marty, the bratwurst kid, shared an equally loud "Amen" of his own, and soon the whole class was shouting it. Sensing the moment was safe amidst the cacophony, Glen let loose the juicy one he'd been holding back all morning. He underestimated its forcefulness, however, and it reverberated far longer and louder than he anticipated. After a moment of inexplicable silence—likely due to shock—Dean yelled, "Hallelujah!" The whole class erupted into side-splitting laughter. Marty, likely inspired by Glen's bold flatulence, added the finishing touch to the raucous spectacle by standing up, and with both arms thrust skyward, yelled, "Praise the LORD!" as a juicy one erupted from within him as well.

Amid the laughter I caught sight of the teacher and was surprised that she did not look mad. She looked disgusted by the flatulence as the smell wafted in her direction, but the laughter and excitement must have helped her endure the farting. I think she was even *happy* about all the noise and enthusiasm—it was probably not something she often elicited from a roomful of teenagers at this hour of the morning. The three of us laughed together in proud admiration of what we had contributed.

The class concluded and we made our way to the hallway, giving and receiving high fives like we had just scored an upset over an opposing team, only to be engulfed by another crowd that had formed around us in the hallway. Marty and countless others were asking who we were and if we'd be back next week. We answered that it was a one-time visit, as far as we knew. What happened next made us immediately second guess that statement.

"Tom! Tom! Get over here!" The request was

from one of the prettiest girls I had ever seen, and that included Samantha Reck. This was not new territory for us; I had seen plenty of pretty girls throw themselves at Tom before. What *was* new, however, was Tom welcoming her attention and waving her over to join us. Glen, Dean, and I formed an immediate offensive line and cleared the way for Tom to head in her direction so that he would hopefully introduce us.

"Oh, hey! How's it goin'?" Tom asked.

"What in the world just happened? Your class was *so loud* today!"

"Yeah, it was pretty funny," Tom said.

She looked at Tom and then at us. Tom looked at us and then at her, completely confused. She rolled her eyes and stuck out her hand to me.

"Aren't you going to introduce me to your friends, Tom?"

Tom started to explain that we were doing a class project together and that we were going to make a movie about overthrowing Hitler, and a bunch of other plot points that blurred together because I temporarily forgot where I was. By the time I came to, names had been exchanged but none of them had registered.

"Nice to meet you," she said sweetly, looking only at me, as if I was the only person there.

"N–nice to meet you, too," Glen, Dean, and I all managed to stammer. She was still staring at me when her equally hot friends magically appeared.

"Can't wait to see your movie! Maybe we can get together and watch it?" the first girl asked Tom. *I can't believe she is still staring at me.* I was falling helplessly into the void of space, like jettisoned trash from a spaceship.

One of the newly arrived girls asked if there was any *romance* in our movie, giggling the whole time. Glen, Dean, and I watched the girls and Tom interact in utter astonishment. My eyes bulged out of their sockets as one of them deliberately touched Tom's arm.

Romance? In a class project? A class project with us four guys and one girl? Samantha's face suddenly popped into my mind, and I felt sweat droplets erupting out of my pores. Dean, Glen, and I exchanged bewildered glances. Not only were we talking with *three* extremely cute girls, but they were flirting with Tom Edison and *us. Us* and *Tom Edison.* I swear the first girl we met still hadn't taken her eyes off me. I could hear the faint tune of *The Twilight Zone* theme music playing alongside my internal screaming.

I returned from my brief daydream to see Tom looking at me expectantly. It dawned on me that someone, probably one of these cute girls, just asked a question and they were awaiting my answer.

"Ahh, well. It's kind of… ah—" I began to say, scrambling for something coherent.

Sensing his wing man had just flown through some jetwash and was spinning out of control, Dean came to my rescue.

"All the parts are cast, sorry. It's a class project," he answered suavely. "But we will keep you in mind for any future projects!"

Leading up to meeting Tom's three good-lookin' friends from church, Glen, Dean, and I rarely had positive interactions with cute girls. In fact, the three of us each had our own quirks.

Glen usually acted indifferent, which was perceived as him playing hard to get. Sometimes girls took his indifference as an invitation to throw themselves at him, but he never returned their affection. When Dean and I replicated the "hard to get" method, our attempts were futile, as girls—who must have intuitive superpowers—could immediately see through our pretenses. But Glen truly wasn't interested. He was singularly focused on earning the love of my sister; he was completely convinced she would come around once we were old enough that the age difference wouldn't matter. He might have grown impatient and moved on had we never watched the movie *The Sandlot*—a story which included this exact happily-ever-after ending between the smoke show lifeguard, Wendy Peffercorn, and a much younger, nerdy deviant, nicknamed "Squints." Glen argued his chances were much higher given that he was the opposite of Squints—at least a hundred pounds heavier, and freakishly strong, too. I secretly agreed with him, which made me even more annoyed.

Dean tended to be shy around girls. He'd

either fumble with his words or poorly try to copycat something suave that a movie character did. In addition to a lack of self-confidence, I was in my head too much—thinking, plotting. Dean didn't have a problem speaking up, and he certainly made attempts to sound cool, but what came out of his mouth usually missed its mark. Glen, on the other hand, had no inner filter and just said whatever came to mind. Sometimes his filter-free approach missed wide, and other times his words were dead-on accurate. I tended to overthink everything, which resulted in missing the moment and standing frozen in place.

In short, I was a hot mess when it came to girls. My preferred method was to just hang out of sight and pray the other two would be successful enough for me to come in on the second wave. How Tom handled himself around girls was in another stratosphere than the three of us. He didn't seem the least bit rattled at school, and at church he appeared to have things under control in a different way. I was jealous of Tom's total lack of nerves around the fairer sex.

The arrival of Tom's friends made "operation girlfriend" a bit more complicated. I may have been the first to profess my interest in Samantha, but Dean had made it clear he intended to sweep her off her feet as well. Sharing a crush on Samantha never bothered me before. Samantha was the princess at the tippity-top of the mountain, and Dean and I were among dozens of hopeful knights in (not so) shining armor.

Any edge one could gain became paramount. I was hopelessly in love with Samantha, just like everybody else in our grade, but when my plan to form the group I wanted was successful, I grew thoroughly convinced it would be me over Dean and everyone else in the end.

Battling my best friend for the girl of my dreams didn't seem like it would end well for either of us. And yet, these thoughts of fighting Dean over Samantha were pushed aside as she suddenly ceased to be the only girl in the picture. Now we had Tom's friends to consider. Unlike Samantha, they didn't yet know anything about us, and for reasons unknown, one of them appeared genuinely interested in me. This was both exciting and terrifying, for I had never been in that position before—with an actual girl so blatantly showing interest in me—and I suspected that neither Glen nor Dean would have any idea what to do either. My world was flipping upside down. This surprise development had me wondering if maybe this was our chance to start fresh and not only do something different but *become* something different— to reach heights we never would have dared. Perhaps I wasn't a hopeless case, after all.

As Tom led the way, Dean, Glen, and I dropped back for a quick debrief before heading into the sanctuary.

"That's *three* cute girls Tom is friends with. Plus, Samantha!" Dean hissed in a dull roar.

"Yeah, I know. But I–I can't even *think* right now. This has been the weirdest twenty-four hours," I replied.

"That is one girl for each of us. Maybe it'll make Jessica jealous," Glen said.

"Dude, give up the dream. My sister is *not* available. She told me yesterday she thought you were a pervert."

"Seriously? *She talked about me?*"

***

Upon entering the sanctuary, the first thing I noticed was that there were people standing shoulder to shoulder, wall to wall. It was the most populated indoor room I'd ever been in. The second thing I noticed was that everyone was singing—*everyone* was singing, and it was loud! This church service was completely different from the ones I was used to, which was intriguing but also unsettling. It was so loud that I couldn't hear myself think, let alone sense Glen approaching me. The noise provided the perfect cover for his sneak attack. He and I had been in this battle lately where we targeted the other person's balls in a secret game we called "Nut Tap." The intent was to smack one another in the groin and cause pain, but without anyone else seeing. It was stupid. It was childish. And yet, it was also ridiculously funny and rewarding. So, there I was, a wide-open target as I walked along unguarded. Glen snuck up and intentionally bumped into me, then delivered a swift and destructive smack to my crotch.

"Nut tap!" Glen whispered loudly in my ear as pain swept through the place where the sun didn't shine.

"Fuhhhhhhhhh," I stopped myself short of swearing in church, restraining the word like a teammate holding back the batter charging the mound. I settled for a glare, silently communicating that I would be avenging my nuts when he least expected it.

Dean and Tom were ahead of us as his mom led the way down the center aisle… all the way to the front row. Where I come from, the only people who sat in the front row in church were the chronically late or the pastor's family. Which was when I spotted Mr. Edison on stage, looking in our direction and wearing an enormous grin.

"Good to see you! Welcome!" Mr. Edison shouted over the singing.

Tom Edison was a pastor's kid?! Of all the possibilities, no one had ever thought of that. I smiled back and waved, and then looked over at Tom, who was conveniently looking somewhere else. The song concluded and Mister—or rather—*Pastor* Edison instructed everyone to sit down.

The church service was different, but it wasn't completely foreign to me. My parents talked with each other about sermons, and I've picked up enough from listening to them to be able to hold my ground when spiritual topics came up. Dean and I never talked about this stuff, but for some reason Glen wasn't uptight about religion, despite having no exposure to it at home. He was curious about my beliefs, and we shared some conversations from time to time—whenever I could get him to stop harassing me about my sister. And now there was Tom's stance to figure out. It seemed like most the people here preferred a house of worship fit for Ned Flanders and family, but Tom appeared to be somewhere in the middle; he wasn't totally enthralled, but neither did he seem dismissive. I could tell that Dean was uncomfortable, but not altogether miserable. I felt uncomfortable, too, but mostly because of information overload from how different and new everything was. Then there was Glen, who seemed to be loving every minute. He was enamored, utterly *astounded,* by the spectacle.

After we sat down, Glen leaned over Dean to say something to me, and I instinctively protected my crotch and leaned away from him. He stifled his laughter as he retreated. I looked Tom's way again, and this time he met my gaze with a shrug of his shoulders and sheepish smile. Before he could say something, Mrs. Edison redirected his gaze to the stage as his dad continued speaking. Soon we were on our feet singing again. By the time Mr. Edison started preaching it was past lunchtime, but I was too entranced to notice my rumbling stomach.

Sure, his sermon was longer than I was accustomed to at my family's humble church, but it was really good. I normally had trouble listening to anything lasting longer than ten minutes—but Tom's dad had me locked in for the full forty or so minutes that he spoke. I loved all his stories and the way he used his stop-motion animation skills to add some lighthearted flare.

The message was about his favorite story of Jesus—the one where he walked on water. Apparently, the disciples all thought he was a ghost, except Peter, who knew it was Jesus and then tried walking on water towards him. Mr. Edison used words like *courage* and *faith* and encouraged us to trust God and keep our eyes on Jesus. I thought it had been thoroughly captivating. I was curious if Tom cared about his faith as much as his parents did. I was hopeful Tom's beliefs were not the extremist kind. He still hadn't shared much about himself, which was a little weird, but also kind of mysterious and cool. What else was there to know about him?

***

"Slow down, slow down, Tom's dad is a pastor? Tom has *several* girlfriends? Sounds like you guys had quite the adventure!" My mom did her best to keep up as I spilled the beans about our sleepover at Tom's.

"I'm glad you three are taking the time to get to know Tom, even if it is for a school project. I've been wondering about him and his family. I didn't know they were so involved in ministry, either. But I think there are worse things a boy could be keeping secret from his classmates," she said.

"You're right. So far, he's pretty cool and fun to be around, even if his mom is—"

She gave me "the look" that dared me to complete my sentence. I decided to let it go. My mom continued to tidy up the kitchen before moving into the living room to pick up where she left off with her scrapbooking. I could hear Jessica in her room with her door closed and *my* music blaring. I was eagerly waiting for my dad to get home so I could fill him in on Tom and all the ideas we had for our class project about WWII. I knew my dad would have lots more for us to think about—he was, after all, the reason I was so into movies.

When I started middle school two years ago, my dad gave me a list of the top 100 movies of all-time that I needed to see before I left for college. I was over halfway through the list, and I hadn't even started high school. The last movie from the list that I saw was *The Bridge on the River Kwai*, so I couldn't have been happier that Mr. Larson gave us WWII as the topic for our group project.

I spent most of the next few weeknights working on a script and plotting over the phone with Dean, Glen, and Tom for the upcoming weekend's production. Samantha said she would help with whatever we needed, but that she trusted us to figure out the details. We planned for Tom to pick up our school-issued camcorder Thursday so that we could do some recording on Friday right after school, then all-day Saturday, and have Sunday as a back-up recording day if we needed it.

I started to anticipate Samantha pulling me aside on Sunday and telling me how much she *loved* working with me and how she hoped we would stay in touch over summer break. I envisioned her writing her phone number down for me, stressing that I could call her *any* time, and how we'd talk about our awesome movie and how the project had been the beginning of something really special between us.

***

Our Media Arts class was abuzz on Friday with chatter about plans as all the groups worked independently on their projects. While Samantha was talking with some friends on the other side of the classroom, I was lost in thought about one of the scenes we'd been attempting to configure. A question about Simon broke my concentration.

"Hey Steve, did you hear about Shorty – er – Simon?" asked a kid from the group Simon was assigned to.

I looked up at him and shook my head.

"He was suspended!" he hissed.

At this, Dean, Glen, and Tom stopped what they were doing and listened, urging the kid to continue.

"At our first group meeting, Belinda set him off—and then she complained to her parents, and *they* complained to Principal Ganley," he elaborated.

"What happened?" I asked.

"He pushed her down. But it was mild, man. Let's just say there was a lot of acting—and the camcorder wasn't even on. I was able to get him into a closet until he calmed down," he said.

"Belinda," I said through clenched teeth.

"Yeah, I know. She told us that her parents badgered Mr. Ganley until they got him suspended—"

"That sucks!" Tom and Glen said.

"Poor guy, now he's definitely gonna need summer school—*again.* I hate dealing with his outbursts, but the guy really doesn't deserve any of this… I feel so bad for him," he concluded, shaking his head as he walked away.

There was a long drawn out pause as we digested the information.

"We could probably talk to Mr. Ganley and Mr. Larson and let Simon be in our group," Tom said.

"No," I said.

"No? What do you mean? It's *Simon,* man," Glen asked.

"No. He's not our problem to deal with this time," I added.

"Damn dude, that's ice cold," Dean said, repressing a small smile, and joining me to my right as we sat opposite Tom and Glen.

"He doesn't deserve suspension or summer school, Steve, and you know it," Glen said.

"Maybe not, but I've – we've – finally got

some distance, *and* a good thing going here—I don't want him around, alright?"

"But—" Glen persisted. Tom appeared to be in Glen's corner, while Dean appeared to be in mine.

"No, *that's it*, ok? He wasn't assigned to our group and I'm not about to undo everything so he can make my life miserable again," I pouted.

Just then Samantha returned to our group and sat down between Glen and I, ending the debate. She looked back and forth between us, sensing the tension.

"What did I miss?" she asked.

"Nothing!" Dean and I shouted in unison, jockeying for her attention simultaneously. My conscience was on fire by this time, but I shoved it aside and did my best to busy myself with writing our script.

***

We agreed to meet at Tom's house an hour after school. My sister said she'd pick Glen, Dean, and me up and drive us there. As the Oldsmobile family car came into view, Glen pushed his way ahead of Dean and me.

"Well, hello there Jessica!" Glen said as he slid into the front passenger seat.

"Ugh, hi Glen," Jessica said, trying (and failing) not to smile.

"I guess we're sitting in the back again, Dean," I said.

"You know, pretty soon you will have your *own* car to drive us everywhere," Glen joked, affecting the deeper voice of an adult in a ridiculous attempt to sound mature.

"Dream on, Glen," Jessica said as we pulled away.

"Yes, I plan to," Glen said, then turned around and made an obscene gesture with his hand.

***

I was finding it peculiarly enjoyable to watch everyone read through the script that I'd whipped up. I watched their faces with great satisfaction as they went from smiling to confused to smiling again. Tom was the most fun to watch. He studied the script with a look of surprised intensity.

"Are you sure I should be shooting someone with a *paintball* gun?" Tom asked me out of earshot of everyone.

Part of me knew that this was a valid concern. But the paintball gun had been a nonstop source for fun ever since Glen got it for his birthday. And now we had the opportunity to have some more fun *and* get school credit at the same time. I didn't think anyone would object to using it for a scene in which we assassinated Hitler, even though it would not be "historically accurate."

Dean, who played Hitler, had been practicing his German accent for a week, and it was still horrible. I think he realized early on that he wasn't getting it, so he decided to intentionally butcher it just for fun.

"For the record, can I just name how terribly insulting and insensitive it is that you have me, who is Jewish, playing the role of Hitler? Shouldn't *I* be the one shooting him?" Dean asked.

Nobody moved or spoke. We only stared at Dean, contemplating.

"But then you wouldn't get to share with us that excellent German accent of yours," I said.

"Great point. I *am* having a lot of fun watching you squirm, Steve," Dean said.

"Ok, Tom—you are playing the role of Informant X. Right now, it is unknown whose side you're on, but for this scene, you're speaking with your boss, Hitler, who is being set up—which will then result in his death."

"Roger that," Tom said.

"Glen, you're going to be over there, by those cluster of trees, pretending to be one of Hitler's bodyguards."

Out of the corner of my eye, I spied Samantha paying close attention. I didn't usually enjoy feeling watched, but because it was her, it felt amazing. *Be cool Steve, be cool.* Glen cursed in pain and then stuck his head out from behind a tree and waved at me.

Glen was up to something. He was a terrible liar, and his behavior made me suspicious, but I waved it off. I had grown accustomed to Glen marching to his own beat. Not wanting to go into twenty questions with him, after we finished Tom and Dean's dialogue, we moved on to the assassination scene. I had Tom get into position and handed him Glen's paintball gun.

I pulled Dean aside. "Do you know what Glen is doing?"

"You'll see. The more *real* the action, the better, right?" Dean blurted, a sly grin on his face, before darting back to his position. Their conspiring messed with my nerves, but I pressed on.

"Ok, here's how this scene is going to go down: Samantha, you're working with Tom as a double agent, so you'll run away from Tom's hideout over to Dean and whisper in his ear. Then you need to get out of there fast. Tom, as soon as its clear, you will take out the Nazi dictator with a few shots to his chest."

Tom nodded and then put the paintball gun to his shoulder.

"Got it," Samantha said as she walked to her mark.

"Glen, when you see Samantha running away from Dean, that's when you need to start shouting for Hitler to take cover because his life is in danger."

Glen gave me a thumbs up, and then disappeared again behind the trees.

"Action!" I yelled and pressed the record button.

Tom and Samantha shared a brief exchange and then Samantha ran up to Dean, whispered in his ear, and ran away. Dean looked awkward and top heavy as he paced; he was wearing about ten t-shirts to soften the sting where the red paint pellets were supposed to explode. I'd given Tom his cue to start shooting and that once he landed a couple of shots I'd yell "cut." This proved to be crucial, but hilarious, oversight.

Once Samantha was out of the way, and just before Tom pulled the trigger, there was a loud hiss followed by a series of violent popping sounds—all coming from the woods near Glen. Glen yelled for the Fuhrer to take cover because his life was in danger— and then all hell broke loose. For a split second, the noise was so loud it really *did* feel like our lives were in danger. The disruption caused me to jump and for Tom to fire away. I wasn't far from Tom, but the popping sounds coming from Glen's area drowned everything out. It soon dawned on me that the extra noise wasn't gunfire, but *firecrackers*. Unable to see or hear me and no doubt feeling like he was in an actual war zone, Tom continued to fire a steady stream of paintballs out of the gun, peppering Dean's body head to toe.

The scene lasted a minute, but it felt much longer. After the firecrackers ended, I zoomed in on the smoky residue they left behind, then zoomed out to capture Dean's body on the ground. The only sounds were the empty clicks of the paintball gun,

Tom's finger *still* pulling the trigger. He had unloaded the entire chamber of paintball ammo on Dean, who was flat on his back and motionless.

"Cut!" I yelled, setting down the camcorder and running over to check if Dean was still alive.

Tom's aim was incredibly accurate. Dean was plastered in paint. There was very little of Dean's clothing that was spared Tom's marksmanship. Dean had endured *several* direct hits to his chest, stomach, legs, neck, and to his *crotch*. If ever there were a fate that Hitler deserved, I'd just captured it on our school-issued camcorder in the woods with my buddies.

Tom, Samantha, and I gave Dean some space to recover, and returned to Tom's house, eager for Glen's return from the woods with some answers. Glen approached soon after, giddier than I'd ever seen him, carrying a duffel's worth of spent fireworks with a multicolored and clearly sore Dean in tow. Dean grimaced and walked up to me gingerly and nodded to Samantha and Tom who repeatedly asked if he was okay.

"Tell me you got it, Steve," Dean whimpered.

"Every. Second," I said as I patted him softly on the back.

After the dust settled on our wild Friday afternoon of moviemaking, Dean blurted, "How's about we go out to the movies tonight?"

"Yes! Great idea!" I exclaimed.

"Uh, I don't know. I was planning to meet up

with my friends from church, but—"

"Are you kidding me? *Yes,* they can join us!" Dean said before Tom could finish his sentence.

"I don't know that I can make it, but thanks for inviting me," Samantha said.

"Really? Bummer. Maybe another time," Dean said, glancing over at me, looking resentful at his strike out. He must have waited the whole day to make his move, and by god, he had followed through.

***

Tom's parents agreed to drop us off at the theater, but only after Tom's mom called each of our parents and verified that they were aware we'd be attending a movie in a darkened room with girls present. The way Mrs. Edison spoke made going to the movies together sound so scandalous. When we arrived at the theater, Dean yanked us into a huddle formation and started speaking to us like a quarterback to his teammates.

"Listen, fellas, it's important *the girls* pick the movie, not us. It not only shows them we're gentlemen, but it serves a much higher purpose."

"Higher purpose?" I asked.

"Yes! Trust me. We *have* to make sure that *they* pick it!" Dean whispered excitedly.

I have heard a lot of Dean's ideas over the years. It was Dean's idea when we decided to sun ourselves in my front yard, laying out on Styrofoam mats because I didn't own any reclinable deck chairs.

He thought that getting a tan would be a great way to impress passerby girls with our physiques on display. We not only scorched ourselves from head to toe, but Jessica and her friends teased us mercilessly. Then there was the time Dean wanted to try smoking, but instead of getting his hands on cigarettes he rolled up brown paper bags and lit one of the ends on fire and we inhaled from the other end. We got into huge trouble for that one. The worst part was that we hadn't actually done anything wrong, other than reek like smoke. Our parents didn't believe our story, because well, I guess the thought never occurred to them that we were too chicken to try the real thing. And then there was that time Dean wanted to prank his brother Jacob, so we dropped Mentos into a two-liter bottle of Coke. That idea literally blew up in our faces, not Jacob's. But Dean's idea about the girls picking out the movie sounded intriguing and relatively risk-free. I nodded my approval to proceed.

"Let's say they are in the mood to laugh, and they pick a comedy, right? What that *really* means is that they want to laugh so hard that they touch your arm, or your leg—"

Glen and I exchanged glances and started to laugh.

"—and if they want to see a *drama*, that means they want to *cry* and be comforted—by *us* of course."

He started to speak faster and more passionately.

"Now, if they want to see a *scary* movie…."

Dean beamed. "*That* means they will want to be comforted *and* protected. If they choose a scary movie, that's because they *want us*. That's a flare in the night sky as a signal that they *want* to be so scared that they jump into our laps! So, if you want to know what they're thinking, then we just keep our mouths *shut* and let them pick!" Dean concluded, sticking out his chest.

"It's not the dumbest thing I've ever heard," I said.

The sight of three girls, each one as attractive as the next, made my heart temporarily stop as they piled out of a car in front of the theater. The girl who didn't stop looking at me when we first met at Tom's church got out of the car last. As soon as she closed the car door, her eyes were on me *again*. I snapped to attention. It was time to put Dean's strategy to the test.

*** *** ***

As we walked toward the girls, who were huddled by themselves, a woman and a man crossed our path, and we couldn't help overhearing them.

"That was the scariest movie I've ever seen," said the woman.

"I know! I can't believe you jumped into my lap!" said the man, laughing.

Glen asked them what they had seen, and they answered, "*Chosen Death*."

We walked over to where the girls were standing.

"What do you want to see?" Tom asked.

"We can't decide. You're the moviemakers, so why don't *you*?" said the girls in unison.

Do they know about Dean's theory too? As if that wasn't disarming enough, the girl with eyes only for me was smiling broadly, her eyes glimmering with – with *what,* I could not register, because a girl had never looked at me like that before. Was that what *desire* looked like? Was I honestly becoming more enamored with her than I was with Samantha? *Why does she keep looking at me like that?*

"No, really. You three get to choose. We're okay with seeing whatever—" I started.

"*Chosen Death*!" Dean blurted.

Glen, Tom, and I whipped around and glared at Dean. He shrugged.

"Ooooh! Sounds scary!" said the girl with glimmering eyes—a girl I desperately wished I had a name for.

Dean smiled knowingly at us in that "I told you so, now watch and learn" look of his. I pulled him aside before we entered the theater.

"Hey, what the hell happened to letting *them* pick?" I asked.

"Sorry. I–I just wanted to make sure!"

We let the girls walk ahead of us like the gentlemen that we were, allowing them to choose their seats before us, which suddenly seemed like a missed opportunity in strategic planning. Thankfully, they sat down with a space in between each of them. Tom acted quickly and took a seat at the end of the row, which left Dean and I standing motionless, contemplating. Before either of us acted, Glen budged past us in his nonchalant way and plopped down in the first available seat. What remained was *girl-open seat-girl-open seat*. Dean made his move a split second before I did, making a beeline for the open seat that was between *two girls*—including the girl with the glimmering eyes. I was struck with instant regret, mad with myself for hesitating. I deliberately stepped on his heels to communicate my dissatisfaction as I followed him down the row. He stopped abruptly and attempted a nut tap, which I barely deflected. He winked at me after he sat down, inspiring me to step on his foot as hard as I could. His stifled welp gave me temporary satisfaction as I took my seat. I glared at him while opening my bag of Twizzlers. I could read his thoughts in that moment, and they were, "Snooze you lose Steve-o."

"Hi, Steve. I'm Jenny."

"Hi, Jenny, nice to meet you," I said. *Oh, thank God* I thought. *At least I know one of their names*. I caught Dean staring in my direction, but not at me, instead, he was looking over my head—and his eyes had grown to the size of saucers.

"Hey guys!" said a familiar voice.

Samantha? Oh, dear God....

"I got out of my plans and was able to make it!

I found Glen in the concessions line and then went and bought my ticket," she said as she sat down at the end of the row… to my immediate right.

Samantha on one side, and Jenny on the other. And on the other side of Dean and Jenny was the girl with glimmering eyes. *This is not happening, this is not happening, this is not happening!*

"Who are the girls? Tom's friends?"

"Yes!" I replied, a little too enthusiastically. I prayed she would introduce herself so I could learn the other two girls' names. Instead, she spotted my Coke and Twizzlers.

"Oooh, I love Twizzlers! I like to use them as a straw."

"Sure!" I said.

Enthusiasm still too high, I had jumped the gun and assumed Samantha had asked to share. I prayed the awkward interchange would end swiftly. I stared at her, mind blank, not even sure what year it was. *Cool it, Harding, cool it….*

"I guess that means you're willing to share?" she giggled as she reached for my Twizzlers and stuck a cherry licorice straw into my Coke, then planted her lips over it for a sip. Phew! My awkwardness hadn't ruined things.

Just as the lights dimmed, there was a commotion next to Dean. The girl with glimmering eyes was getting up! And she was swapping seats with Jenny! *Is this happening?* She settled into her new seat and looked me square in the eyes.

"I couldn't see over the guy in front of me and Jenny is taller than I am," she said, taking one of my Twizzlers, too. My mind was racing, unable to process any of this. Samantha was on my right. *Oh dear Lord*, I thought, as *The Twilight Zone* theme music started up in my head. I looked over at Dean, who was shaking his head incredulously at me. I tried unsuccessfully not to smirk. He flipped me the bird. I smiled, then glued my eyes to the screen. I, Steve Harding, was at the movies sitting between two girls I had active crushes on. I waited for my instincts to kick in, but it was radio silence within. I felt no nudges, no inner guidance. I was flying blind. I had no idea what to do, so I decided not to do anything.

I had seen a lot of movies in my life, and I remembered almost every single one of them—but that night it was obvious from the start that I would not recall a single frame from this movie. That woman leaving the theater must have been right, *Chosen Death* seemed like the scariest movie ever. Moviegoers were screaming, jumping, clinging to others. Not this guy. I sat utterly shell-shocked, filled with inexplicable peace and calm for the length of the movie, feeling more alive and joyous than ever before. I could turn my head one way and smell Samantha's perfume, and then turn the other way and it was the same perfume, but on a different girl—a girl I desperately wanted to know the name of, but didn't. I didn't dare look at Dean, and thankfully Glen was far enough down the row.

To my tremendous shock, my female seatmates followed Dean's theory to the letter. They touched my arm, put their faces onto my shoulders, and they even grabbed my entire torso. I kept worrying they were going to headbutt each other. It was the stillest I had ever been—I was probably more motionless than when sleeping. Neither girl seemed to notice the other. It was like they both owned the same teddy bear—and that teddy bear was *me!* My body served as their personal scare pillow. I wondered if either of them was aware how torturous each touch was. If they could read my thoughts, they would have been confused, because I had to imagine Michael Jordan and Scottie Pippen dunking on opponents to keep from pitching a tent right then and there. I managed to keep calm and my loins inconspicuous, despite hearing Glen's voice in my head saying, "Boner alert, three o'clock!"

There's no doubt that having two girls unable to keep their hands off me was arousing. Thinking of my favorite basketball players had successfully kept the fire from getting out of control. And yet, as turned on as I was, I was also just very, very happy. I had somehow outdone even myself—the guy who never stopped thinking and dreaming. The Steve-Harding-sandwich during the movie sparked something within—I was ready for anything. For the first time in my life, I felt fearless, invincible, even.

When the lights came back on, Glen insisted that the girls exit the row first. As each filed past him, they patted him on the back, thanking him for his chivalry. Next, we gathered in the lobby and debriefed the movie while waiting for our parents to pick us up. We managed to quietly ask Tom to refresh the girls' names for us. Then I learned that moments after Dean gave me that bragging look, he'd tried to put his arm around Victoria, my glimmering-eyed girl. He said the look on her face was enough to promptly remove his arm, but the damage had been done. One minute later, she was on the move because of her "inability to see the screen." It dawned on me that perhaps the best thing I could have done was not try to do anything. Perhaps that meant my instincts were right all along! All I had to do was just be as still as a teddy bear.

Victoria asked what I thought of the movie, but I dodged and asked Tom.

"I loved it!" Tom said with a huge smile.

"It was the scariest thing *I've* ever seen!" Victoria yelled.

"What about you Samantha, what did you think?" Tom asked.

"I had to shield my eyes for most of it," she replied. "But thanks to Steve, I somehow managed. I don't know how he did it, but he didn't even flinch!" Samantha gushed. I averted my eyes to the floor as she looked in my direction.

"Right?!" Victoria added enthusiastically, and they teamed up and playfully pushed me. I was on cloud nine and couldn't help but smile and shrug.

"Dude! Way to go! You're the man!" Glen said triumphantly next to me.

I could have accepted Glen's accolades and basked a bit longer in the moment, but then I noticed that he and I were behind the pack and out of sight from onlookers. Leaning over to Glen, I patted him on the shoulder and thanked him—and then paid his unguarded nuts some revenge.

"Nut tap!"

***

Saturday dawned, and we found ourselves at Samantha's house, where we had chosen to finish our project. This was a part of town with lakeshore properties and three-car garages we dubbed "mansion city." Her house was loaded with electronics: a kick ass stereo system, the largest television I had ever seen, and an endless vinyl and CD collection. There was also a baby grand piano in the living room.

We set our things down and began to look for places to film our first scene of the day when I heard the faint sound of a door opening somewhere on the second floor.

"Oh, that's my obnoxious younger brother, Barry, who I was telling you about. He will probably harass us like he usually does when I have friends over. But he won't be able to bother us *all* day—one of his friends is picking him up around two o'clock."

Clearly eavesdropping on our conversation and his sister's introduction, Barry then appeared at the top of the steps in full view of everyone.

"Hey dorks! Check it out!" his high-pitched voice beckoned.

Right in front of all of us, this kid bent over and pulled down his pants, exposing a pair of white and hairless butt cheeks—a full moon at noon.

"Barry! Gross!" Samantha yelled.

"Let me introduce you to Hugh Jassman," retorted Barry.

We looked to Glen, our threat neutralizer, to put an end to Barry.

"Hey kid, do you know what a purple nurple is? Why don't you come on down and try one on?" Glen asked.

"No thanks!" Barry said, pulling up his pants and walking away. He went into his bedroom and closed the door. Then he opened the door and made a raunchy fart sound by pressing his mouth against his hands and pushing air into them.

I was half amused and half angry with Barry. On the one hand, his artificial farting efforts were hilarious. Afterall, I *had* asked for a "fart machine" for Christmas in the not-too-distant past. On the other hand, this little punk was intruding on our plans and was quickly becoming a distraction. Samantha had tried to give us fair warning, telling us he would be around when she extended the invitation to meet at her house. In hindsight, we should have heeded that warning. But just as I had spaced out when meeting Tom's friends at church, I think I became agreeable to anything the moment Samantha opened her mouth. She could have invited us over while warning us about our imminent deaths, and we would have happily accepted. *Toxic waste? Sure! Giant sinkhole? No problem. Annoying younger brother with nothing better to do? Absolutely.*

I hoped he had gotten his attempts at disruption out of his system and that would be all. But if Barry was capable of unashamedly mooning us within the first five minutes of our arrival, it was evident he was not just going to be a minor inconvenience—he was a potential project killer. And that possibility ignited something deep within. For the first time in my life, I was feeling *passionate* about something. I wanted to finish what was turning out to be an awesome story. Barry's presence felt like an intrusion of the worst kind. Instead of shaking it off or seeking escape, I was going on the offensive, prepared to complete this project at all costs. I felt like I was a rabid mother bear with a case of spontaneous explosiveness disorder that had been triggered by my cubs (my moviemaker groupmates) becoming endangered. Finishing this project successfully had become *that* important to me, and I wasn't about to let this obnoxious brat stand in the way.

"So, what kind of movie are you guys making with my sister? Is it something *girly*?"

"It's a World War two thriller. Now will you

please leave us alone?" I asked point blank.

Barry shrugged and walked back into his room.

"He just likes attention, but he's harmless," Samantha said after the sound of Barry's door closed.

"So, what are we doing today?" Samantha asked.

"We have a lot of ground to cover, beginning with some action sequences between Tom and me," I explained.

"Oh, really?" Samantha asked. "What kind of action do you mean?"

"A fight scene," I said.

Our excitement for the day's events bubbled up as we poured over the outline I had prepared. Reading through it and sharing laughs and playful jabs, I had just started giving myself over to a sense of hopefulness when the sound of the doorbell erased my ease.

Barry thundered down the steps toward the door. Our talking quieted as we sat paralyzed in curiosity and trepidation. Barry whipped open the door and there stood his friend, grinning ear to ear.

A wave of relief washed over me as we watched Barry go out and close the door behind him. *Ding dong, the wicked witch is dead!*

"I've got a funny feeling my brother isn't going to the park," Samantha said.

"What? For real? He isn't leaving?" the four of us yelled over each other.

"I don't think so. He does this all the time. He's probably out there right now dismissing his friend's mom so they can sneak up on us."

Sweat began to form on my forehead. I stuffed down my dread and anger as best as I could and focused on the task at hand.

***

Since we had killed Dean's character the day before, I put him in charge of the camcorder and directing. He made Tom and me take our places. I looked nervously around, anxious for Barry and his friend to spoil the scene. As far as I could tell, the coast was clear. It was just us and mother nature.

"Action!" Dean yelled.

Just as we were beginning our short dialogue exchange, there was a loud farting sound coming from somewhere behind us. Everyone stopped and looked around at one another. Like I said, I was a sucker for fake fart noises like any other adolescent, but this time only Barry and his friend were laughing.

We did our best to ignore the intruders, who had clearly found their expert timing hilarious. Once their laughter died out, I hoped against all hope that they had moved on.

"Action," Dean said in a whisper.

Once again, the scene was interrupted by Barry's loud, fake flatulence, followed by a fit of cackling.

"Knock it off, Barry!" Samantha yelled.

We went through this another six or seven times, each time getting spoiled by Barry and his farting. And then an epiphany struck me. Before I had a chance to filter the thought, I yelled toward Barry and his friend, who were hiding behind the side of the house.

"Hey Barry, we are getting to the good stuff now and we could use your help!"

Dean, Glen, and Tom glared at me. Samantha's jaw dropped.

Barry hushed his friend and poked his head out.

"Say what?" Barry yelled back.

"We are doing a fight scene. You two want to be in it?"

Without consulting his friend, Barry walked in our direction.

"Yes!"

I continued.

"Tom, how do you feel about letting these guys rough you up a little?"

"Uh, what?" Tom asked, his voice rising.

The insight came to me in an instant. The phrase, *if you can't beat them, join them*, was reverberating off the insides of my skull. We still had to get through this scene, despite Barry's antics. And since we couldn't tie him up somewhere without getting his sister in trouble, we would have to *include* him, as detestable as the thought was. Thankfully, it was an action scene, and there were no lines for them to predictably butcher for their own twisted pleasure and our ruin.

"Barry, why don't you and your buddy get in there and do your best to take Tom down—just kind of shove him to the ground and—"

"Yeah, yeah, yeah, I want to be a stunt double when I grow up," Barry yelled, waving me off.

"Tom, just roll with it. Just let them push you around a bit, and then our fight scene will pick up where they leave off."

Tom laughed, "I wasn't exactly sure I was down with *you* punching me, and now you want me to… get beat up by *these two?*"

"We won't really beat you up. I've seen what the stuntmen do. We got this," Barry assured Tom, looking at me with an abundance of self-confidence.

"Are. You. Mental?" Dean hissed, careful to make sure no one else could hear him.

"Would you rather they keep farting?"

"No. But, are you really going to, you know, include these two dorks in our movie?"

"Do you have a better idea?" I asked.

Dean looked at me and then over at Barry and his friend, who were already rehearsing their moves, and then back at me. He shrugged and smiled.

What transpired after that was nothing short of Oscar-worthy. Barry and company throttled Tom with a series of fake punches and kicks, with every single one appearing to land, even though they hadn't. Tom didn't really know how to take fake punches, but the look on his face sufficed—he wasn't acting scared—he *was* scared. I could tell that they must have been movie buffs like us because he and his buddy had quite the fighting choreography all worked out. It was an epic battle and thankfully, Dean captured it all on video.

"Cut!" Dean yelled. "Wow! That was amazing!"

Barry beamed. We exchanged high fives with them and then they left us to go to the park. Samantha accompanied them since Barry's friend's mom wasn't there to drive them.

"I can't wait to watch what you guys film while I'm gone!" Samantha called over her shoulder as they walked away.

We had one more fight scene to do, and then only the final scene to film after and we'd be done. Glen had a lot of opinions about the last fight sequence; he was adamant the camcorder needed to stay in the fray to make it look more realistic. Dean wanted to stay safely out of reach as Tom and I got into it, but Glen insisted that Dean move closer, and Dean ultimately relented. We choreographed and practiced all the punches and kicks until we felt we were ready to try with the camcorder rolling.

Dean yelled "Action!" Tom and I wasted no time going at each other. A week ago, this was the scene I was most looking forward to, but probably for the worst reasons—I wanted to neutralize Tom and show off my strength to Samantha. But now, I wasn't sure Samantha was the girl I should be going for, and neither girl was here right now anyway. So, I held back from demonstrating the full extent of my power, opting to focus strictly on my "acting." Tom, on the other hand, seemed to be digging deep and tapping into some force I had not expected from him. His energetic output was lively and fierce—and contagious. I found my energy and intensity rising to meet his.

Tom spun out of the way and threw a perfectly placed punch, just grazing my chin. It was so close I audibly groaned and winced. Next, it was my turn to be on the offensive. I grabbed Tom's head and thrust him into a headlock. Dean rushed in, practically shoving the camcorder lens into Tom's face. He was incredibly close… too close, in fact, because when Tom twisted out of the lock and went for the knock-out punch, the camera's proximity was so distracting that I failed to react fast enough, and Tom's punch landed right on my nose. The blow caused me to reel forcefully into Dean, knocking him and the camcorder to the ground.

Everyone rushed over to us. Dean stood quickly and he and the others formed a huddle around me. I sat up and rubbed my nose before slowly getting to my feet again. When I smiled, they cheered.

"Whoa! That was incredible!" Glen yelled. "You two are like action stars in the making!"

I felt jubilant. It was the performance of a

lifetime. This project was truly going to be the culmination of all our efforts and without a doubt the best one in the class. I could envision the applause now, and Samantha's adoring gaze….

"Uh, Steve?" Dean asked.

"Please don't tell me you didn't get all of that, Dean."

"The camcorder is broken."

***

"I swear to God, Dean, if you tell me to shut it off and turn it on again, I am going to shove this camcorder so far up your—" I spat.

"I'm telling you, it works when *Zelda* freezes!" Dean interrupted.

"That may work with your Nintendo, but trust me, I can hear something rattling inside it. It won't work, it's not powering up at all. Something is seriously wrong. It's broken, okay? Game over," I declared.

"Can we at least try to get the tape out? We were practically finished," pled Dean.

"I don't know if we should try that and risk making it worse. What if we get the tape out but ruin it in the process?"

"We're screwed either way guys," Glen chimed in. "Where are we going to find a replacement camcorder on such short notice? This thing is due in two days and right now we have nothing to show."

My anger over the camcorder gave way to sadness and panic, then back again to anger as we continued our debate about our sudden unfortunate predicament. The incident quickly brought out the worst in Dean, Glen, and I as we yelled over one another and pointed fingers about what happened. We were all distraught about our hard work being held hostage in the broken camcorder. I noticed Tom wasn't saying anything, and looked over to see his face was beet red and all screwed up, like he was locked in a battle within himself. Our arguing had just reached a boiling point when Tom lifted his eyes from the ground and spoke.

"We can use my dad's Sony."

There was a moment's confusion before we all remembered Mr. Edison's stop-motion hobby and expensive Sony camcorder. That device was electronic craftsmanship which made the school-issued camcorders look like antiques. Mr. Edison's Sony was technically an option, maybe even our *only* option because I didn't have a camcorder, and neither did Glen or Dean.

"He won't need it when he's at church tomorrow. We can meet at my house in the morning—I'll pretend to be sick and stay home. We'd have the whole morning to finish our project and he shouldn't suspect we were even there. What do you say?"

"Holy shit, Tom. That's… that's fuckin' badass," Glen said.

"Won't *our parents* be suspicious though?" I interjected, pointing to Glen and Dean.

"Not if we sleep over at my place tonight. My dad won't think twice about dropping us off at Tom's on a Sunday morning and then picking us up when we're done," Glen said.

We knew that what we were contemplating had the potential to blow up in our faces, but at that point we were all equally passionate about this movie—we *all* had skin in the game. Well, everyone minus Samantha, who we had practically forgotten to include thus far.

"Wait, Tom, that's awesome and all, dude. But don't you think Samantha might have one? Her house is full of top shelf electronics and TV's and stuff. Her parents probably have a camcorder. Shouldn't we ask her first?" chimed Glen. "Oh, look, she's coming back. *Hey, Samantha!*" he started yelling.

Dean grabbed his mouth and shushed him. "Dude, we're going to look like such idiots that we broke the camera while she was gone and need her to bail us out. Let's just use Mr. Edison's camera, we've already got a plan!"

Dean and Glen both started talking over one another, but Samantha was only a few yards away at this point. They both looked at me to settle the matter. I glanced over at Tom, and he seemed uncomfortable and still kind of red-faced, but when our eyes met, he shrugged and nodded. I didn't love the idea of risking all our necks, but I couldn't deny Dean's logic that we looked like dumbasses for breaking the camera while Samantha wasn't there, and it'd be pretty pathetic to need her to fix the situation. I still cared enough to not look that uncool in front of her. Besides, we didn't know that she had a camera to offer anyways.

"Hey guys! How did the scene go? What's going on?" she asked when she reached us.

I gave her a summary of the camera breaking, skating over the argument we'd had about whose fault it was. "So, we're going to film it all again tomorrow using Tom's dad's camera at his house. Samantha, can you make it tomorrow morning, too?" I asked.

"Yes, I think so."

Something shifted in my gut as she said it. I couldn't tell if hearing her voice had unleashed the butterflies, or if her acceptance meant that tomorrow's secret mission at Tom's was officially in motion… it was probably a little of both.

***

Our sleepover at Glen's was uneventful. The three of us were so exhausted and sore after the day's action sequences, and the mood was pretty low with our disappointment about losing everything we'd worked on so far— *and* the realization that we had to do it all over again the next morning. We watched a late-night movie in silence, and I was the first to fall asleep.

We got up as early as we had the morning

after sleeping over at Tom's house, but this time without an overly chipper mom calling us to breakfast as our alarm. We packed up our things without talking, too. I couldn't remember a time when we had gone two minutes without talking during a sleepover, and we were going on twelve hours without a word. It was like we were preparing to jump out of a plane and storm enemy lines, uncertain if we would survive the fight.

Glen's dad drove us to Tom's house, and we arrived just as Samantha's dad was dropping her off. Tom opened the front door and let us in. The house was empty. Glen was the last one down the stairs, having snatched a blueberry pancake from the kitchen on his way. I gave him a disapproving but envious look. He shrugged and tried to nut tap me, but I turned away before he made contact.

"Look at you, quick as a cat this morn!" Glen chided.

"Yeah, yeah. Don't eat with your mouth full – er, don't talk," I retorted, still not fully awake, or used to using my voice again.

"Good one," Glen mumbled over his chewing.

We stood around Mr. Edison's miniature model of the Holy Lands and watched as Tom disengaged the camcorder from its tripod, and then as he meticulously removed the tape and replaced it with a new one.

"Fingerprints, Tom! Leave no trace!" Dean said, breaking the ice.

We laughed as Tom jumped, then abruptly stopped when he bobbled the camcorder.

"Ok, out to the woods to kill Hitler… again," I said lethargically.

Glen revealed his loaded paintball gun and nodded. Dean laughed nervously. We followed the two of them out of Tom's basement door and walked in silence toward the deserted park.

"Sorry, but there will be no enemy fire this time. I used all my firecrackers the first time," Glen said as we arrived at the woods where we recorded just two days before.

I felt an instant wave of disappointment. Friday's scene, although terribly chaotic, was now only a fond memory. I was saddened that I may never get to see how it looked on video, and doubtful about our chances of replicating it.

I called out a monotone "action." We nailed the scene on the first take; Hitler was dead with just three shots to his chest instead of getting lit up like a Christmas tree in the previous version. There was no energy. Even Dean's German accent sounded acceptable. I chalked our bland performance up to the fact that it was a Sunday morning rather than a Friday afternoon, and that we were redoing something that none of us wanted to redo. We made our way back to Tom's house for a break. This time around didn't feel like fun—it felt like *work*—no, it felt like *schoolwork*. By the time we got back into Tom's basement, I'd decided I'd had enough of our plan B.

"This sucks," I said.

"Yeah," everyone replied in unison.

"Do we want to keep at it?" I asked.

"Do we have any other choice?" Dean asked.

I looked around the group and was met with a lot of blank stares and silence. The secret mission excitement had worn off. No one, including me, wanted to keep doing what we had just done the day before. It felt like the air had been sucked out of the room and we were just floating in space, deadened and void of emotion. And then Samantha spoke up.

"I think we should ditch this and do something else."

We looked at her dumbfounded, but curious, and nonverbally urged her to continue her proposal.

"I–I've been memorizing this monologue for an audition I'm doing for the drama club. It's from a play based on *The Diary of Anne Frank*."

I was frozen in place again, unable to move, like an awake Han Solo in carbonite, a mixture of apprehension and openness washing over me. I was still frozen but beginning to thaw.

"Anyway, what we've been doing has been really fun so far, but—I don't think we should keep at it. I'm wondering if you guys are open to doing something completely different instead?"

"Yeah, I am. I mean, I love what we had, but I don't know that it was, uh, something we would've gotten a good grade on," Tom said.

Tom's comment stopped me cold. For the

most part I agreed it was time to make a switch, but his insinuation about the quality of our project stung. It felt like he'd punched me in the nose… again.

"What do you mean, what we had was *incredible*!" Dean fired.

Hearing Dean defending our video affirmed my feelings and reawakened the rabid mama bear within and loosed the chains on my tongue.

"I agree. What we had was like the best stuff we could have asked for. Maybe the redo isn't going to be as great, but it's the only script we have to work with," I added. Dean nudged my shoulder and stood by my side in solidarity. "I worked pretty hard on writing it…" I trailed off, a little embarrassed after having said it. But I *had* worked really hard on it, and knew it was good. I didn't want the one thing I'd finally put effort into in my life to go down the toilet.

"No, no, you're right. We *can* keep going. I was just thinking that we could *try* something else instead, that's all," Samantha said as her face flushed.

"C'mon guys, maybe we should hear Samantha out. Our movie *was* great—but it's just that… I don't think Mr. Larson would—" Tom trailed off as Dean and I dared him to finish his sentence. And then Glen stepped forward and stood beside Tom.

"Tom's right, guys," Glen said. "So, cool your jets and hear him out. He deserves that, don't you think?" Glen said while looking around the basement and at the Sony camcorder in my hands. Glen motioned for Tom to continue.

"Go on, don't worry. We're listening," Glen said, motioning for Tom to continue, while not taking his eyes off Dean and me.

Tom took a breath, and then said, "It's not historically accurate, the first scene was like ten minutes long and we still aren't even done yet, and Samantha is barely in it," Tom said, not making eye contact. "*I* love it, but I don't think… I'm just not sure we want to, uh – keep going with it," he finished.

Dean swore and threw up his arms.

"I can't believe this – this – mutiny," Dean shot at Glen and Tom.

Samantha and Tom stood side by side, quietly looking at the floor. Glen, now on the other side of Tom, had not looked away from Dean nor me. I weighed our options, and it became obvious that our group was divided. The tie-breaking vote was Tom's because he was our assigned leader, and he was already on the hook for the broken camcorder. And, deep down, I hadn't been enjoying anything we'd tried to redo today. I decided to surrender.

"Fine, let's switch gears then," I said.

Dean looked indignant but remained silent.

"It's fifty percent of our grade, and I have a solid C+ right now. We need to bail on this, Dean," I said.

"Alright fine. I guess I'm outvoted. So, what are we going to do instead?"

"We're going to let Samantha take the lead,"

Tom said.

Samantha stepped forward, smiling at Tom, still red-faced. Something about the *way* she smiled at Tom tripped an alarm inside me, and suddenly I *knew* who her first choice for the project had been. I had refused to let myself put those pieces together before, but now it was painfully evident. *She liked Tom*. And in that second, I lost hope for winning over Samantha. Part of me had already let go because of how I felt about Victoria, but part of me had held on because I had liked Samantha for such a long time before I met Victoria.

Above all, I *hated* that Tom was right about what we needed to do for the project. I felt like I was finally proving to be somebody worthy of Samantha's caliber, like I had earned some common ground with her, only to be outshone and overlooked by the class heartthrob once again. As Samantha faced us and started to share her vision, my thoughts whirled out of control and the words spilling out of her mouth became gibberish in my ears.

***

"Wow, that sounds *great*, Samantha. I think we can manage that just fine, don't you think, *Steve*?" Glen's question snapped me out of my thought-tornado.

"Yes, for sure. Totally doable," I replied as confidently as I could, despite once again not registering a single thing she had said.

"That's the spirit!" Glen said and thumped me on the back, knocking all the air out of my lungs.

I looked around the room, trying to see what the others were doing, and nobody was moving. I was utterly lost as to the new plan. All I knew was that Samantha was probably going to recite her Anne Frank monologue. Thankfully, that was apparently all I needed to know.

"Ok, I think it would work best if I recited my monologue in front of that closet door. Then I will walk through it and after the door closes behind me, you can stop recording."

The plan was very simple. Samantha was the title character and the rest of us a concoction of the others Anne shared the hidden space with: Glen was the obnoxious sixteen-year-old Peter, Tom was going to play Anne's dad, I was the dentist who joined later in the story. Dean was insistent on playing a Gestapo. We kept the story mostly the same as history's version, and only modified things slightly for dramatic effect. After all, we still had Glen's paintball gun and wanted to kill at least one Nazi—opting to smoke Dean's character when he discovered the Frank family's hiding place.

"Plan B" turned out to be amazing thanks to the unquestioned star of the production, *Samantha*. Her monologue was nothing short of spectacular. Somehow, she nailed that monologue on the *first take*—and what a take it was! Simply magnificent acting! It was emotionally stirring, especially hearing Anne Frank's story shared in first person. Samantha delivered her part with such natural poise, authenticity, and boldness. The reality of Anne's experience, given voice by Samantha, thoroughly unseated me. In that moment I both appreciated what people like Anne went through and fell in love with Samantha all over again. As mesmerizing as her skin-tingling beauty was, it was the sound of her voice and the revelation of her superb acting ability that were winning my affections for her. All I could do was stand there as she spoke, fully immersed in *Samantha the actress,* as she flawlessly delivered the best speech I had ever heard.

We finished recording our secret mission Plan B in ninety minutes, giving ourselves plenty of time to clean up and cover our tracks. Tom returned his dad's Sony to its tripod, put a fresh tape back in, and helped us finish tidying up the basement. We even dusted our fingerprints off every surface, just in case. Glen's dad picked everyone up, including Samantha, and drove us all to our homes. We were likely in our bedrooms dreamily reminiscing about what had transpired before the Edison's even got home from church.

The next day we eagerly handed in our assignment to Mr. Larson and then spent our class time watching all the group projects. Our project was by far the best—and it wasn't close. The class applauded us, and even made Samantha stand and take a bow for her performance.

"Very impressive, *very* impressive. I was curious how you boys would incorporate Ms. Reck into your group. What a pleasant surprise that she had such a *prominent* role—and what a powerful performance!" Then Mr. Larson gave us our grade— an A+.

"My apologies that your first attempt was ended by the malfunctioning camcorder. None of the other groups reported any problems, but there's always one, isn't there? I will bring it in and see if the guys at Radio Shack can recover anything."

We told him that we had tried turning it off and on again, but nothing seemed to work. He expressed delight when we told him how determined we were, and how Tom's dad let us borrow his camcorder so we could start over and still be able to hand in our assignment on time.

I was still bummed that we'd probably never get to see our original masterpiece again, but everything had gone so smoothly with the Anne Frank filming and ultimately, I was happy with our finished product, and overjoyed about how Samantha had saved the day. That evening, just as I was sitting down for supper, the phone rang.

"Hello?" I answered.

"Hello. Is this Steve?" the caller asked.

"Yes, who's calling?" I asked, unable to pinpoint the familiar voice.

"This is Mr. Edison, Tom's dad. I'd like to

speak with one of your parents, please."

***

"I swear I only fired the one time," Glen pleaded.

"Well, Mr. Edison said he found an exploded paintball somewhere, and when he confronted Tom, Tom spilled the beans and blew our cover story wide open," I said.

"This is not good. Not good at all," Glen said.

"No, it's not. He told my mom that Tom was grounded and that they weren't sure we would be welcome at their house again. And did I ever get a lecture about that!"

"We knew it was a risk, but man, I thought we had been so careful," Glen said.

"Yeah, me too. Well, I better call Dean and fill him in," I said and ended the call.

***

The following day I was eager to get to Media Arts, our last class before school was out, so I could speak with Tom and apologize for what had happened. I didn't want to stay mad at him, and I knew any of us probably would've fessed up, too. I walked into the room and saw Tom talking to Samantha. I instantly felt jealousy churning in my gut like lava. A Metallica song began roaring at a fever pitch in my head. My hands curled into fists. I clenched every muscle. I was so angry tears began forming in the corners of my eyes. All the kindness and sympathy I had been feeling for him vanished. I walked to my desk and sat down, intentionally avoiding eye contact with him. Dean and Glen pulled up their chairs next to me.

"I knew she liked him. I just knew it. Of course, *Tom* would be the one," I seethed under my breath, unable to contain it.

"What are your panties all bunched up about?" Glen chided.

I lifted my chin to indicate where Tom and Samantha sat.

"What's not to like? I think he's cool, too," Glen said nonchalantly. "The guy risked his ass for a stupid school assignment. And now he's paying for it just like we are."

I glared at Glen, unable to attack his logic without revealing what was really bothering me.

"I agree, Steve. He was probably just playing us so he could get to Samantha," said Dean. "Let's TP his house as soon as we're ungrounded."

"Ok class, ok! Time to find your seats," Mr. Larson announced.

Tom sat down and Samantha walked across the room and waved and smiled at the three of us before sitting down. We returned her wave with our own, but my smile wasn't nearly as broad as hers.

"After such terrific video productions, for our last class, I thought we would do some trivia instead of watching a movie like you've probably been doing in all your other classes."

The class groaned their disapproval.

"Ha, I should have known you'd rather have it the other way. Oh well, my mind is made up. Let's have you get into your groups again. You'll need to rely on one another for this doozy of a quiz," Mr. Larson laughed to himself as he turned to the chalkboard and started writing out the questions. The instant Mr. Larson's back was to the classroom, everyone but our group broke out into paper football games and chatted excitedly about summer plans.

Tom and Samantha joined the three of us in the back of the classroom. I decided I'd better act normal rather than pout and look like a wuss. Just then the PA system cracked to life and the voice of the middle school administrator came on:

"Band students are excused to go clean out their band lockers. I repeat, all 8th grade band students are excused to the band room."

Samantha stood up.

"That's me! I will see you guys this summer, right?"

"Yes-hell yes-definitely-for sure!" we all stumbled over one another in reply.

"Awesome! I hope the fallout with your parents goes away soon. I've given Tom my phone number, so if you decide to make any other movies, please let me know!"

I repeated her statement in my head and

couldn't help feeling jealous. Samantha had the hots for Tom and had given *him* her phone number. My blood began to boil. Samantha left the classroom, leaving the four of us to tackle Mr. Larson's trivia challenge, which given his current progress on the chalkboard, wouldn't be starting for at least another twenty minutes. Tom and I caught each other's eye. He smiled weakly.

"So, Tom. How are ya?" Glen gushed, his emphasis and eyebrow-waggling giving Tom an invitation to spill—whether about his grounding or Samantha, I was unsure.

"Been better. Sorry guys. I–I didn't know what to tell him…" Tom muttered.

"Why not tell him you were finger painting to make yourself feel better?" Dean offered sarcastically.

"Yeah, good one. I should have."

"So, you and Samantha, *huh?* When did *that* start?" I asked, unable to hold back my fury.

Tom looked taken aback. His face blushed red, and he looked down at his feet.

"Sorry guys. I – we… I know how much you like her, but—"

"But *what?* You can't help it that you both have the hots for one another? It almost worked out perfectly for you two, *didn't it?* You named her your first choice, and she named you. Match made in heaven," I continued.

"What? No! No, that's not how it went at all, Steve. I swear."

"Whatever. That's fine. We'll live," I said. Dean nodded his head approvingly.

"Dude, I *swear*. That's not at all how things are, man. I don't even—"

"Save it, Tom. Just go out with her and live happily ever after," I fired dismissively.

"I named *you*. *You* were my first choice. I wanted to be in your group because you're—"

"Everybody's friend. Yeah... I know." My rancor was dissipating as his confession registered. I was stunned.

"Well, *yeah*, but – but that wasn't why. I wanted to be in your group because I thought you would be the most fun to work with and probably would make the best project, too."

Tom had chosen *me*, not Samantha. I didn't know what to say. Fortunately, Glen closed the silence, saving me from having to think of an immediate reply.

"Well, no one would blame you if you and Samantha hooked up, Tom. She's beautiful inside and out, man. I still can't stop thinking about that speech she did as Anne Frank."

I thought he was coming to my rescue. Instead, he was giving Tom permission to date the girl of my dreams. My anger kicked up a notch.

"Yeah, thanks, Glen, but – but I don't think that's gonna be happening," Tom said, looking away.

"No, it is not. Because *I* am gonna take that number and Samantha and *I* are going to take our soon-to-be romance to the next level," Dean said as he snatched the piece of paper with Samantha's number on it out of Tom's hand.

Glen and I burst into incredulous, mocking laughter, but Dean stood firm. He wasn't laughing or even smiling.

"Laugh it up, but I am totally serious. If Tom doesn't have the guts to do it, I will," Dean fired.

It dawned on me that Dean was serious. I went from a simmer to a raging, steaming boil.

"The hell you are," I hissed, grabbing for the piece of paper but missing.

"Guys, come on. Cool it. This isn't funny anymore," Glen said.

"Sure, take his side. *Typical*," I said without thinking.

"What did you just say?" Glen asked, his posture shifting from laid back to upright.

"*You heard me*. I am tired of you two forming alliances behind my back—you weren't trying to *help* me with those firecrackers, you were trying to *mess* with me for a laugh!" I shouted.

"Guys, come on—just stop this. It's not worth it," Tom interjected.

"Easy for you to say," Dean snapped.

Sensing an escape to go on the offensive toward Tom and away from Glen, whose anger triggered my instinct to run in the other direction, I jumped on Dean's insult bandwagon.

"Yeah, says the guy *everybody* wants,

including Samantha. But it's back to playing hard to get, isn't it? Isn't that your angle?" The wrath was spewing forth like an uncontained wildfire flaming to life with a gust of wind. I reached for the phone number again and missed.

"You better settle down, Harding. Or I will end you," Glen poked his finger on the last word, and I dodged out of the way.

"Just leave it be, *seriously*. This is not worth fighting about, honestly. Please. Just stop!" There was an urgency in Tom's voice now, and a little voice within advised me to back down. I could hear my conscience trying to get my attention, but I was too far gone. I pressed on.

"*Just leave it be, seriously*," I sneered, mocking him. "What the *hell*, Tom? You've got this secret stash of girlfriends all over you in your other life, and then the one girl I – we – express interest in, you go and get *her* phone number?" I shouted in a whisper that failed to be discreet.

Tom blushed scarlet, a desperate look on his face. "No! You don't understand. You don't get it at all. I–I don't even think I *like* girls that way, okay?!"

I had pushed him too far. I was always proud of myself for never crossing the line—but I just did. And for what? Guilt washed over me as tears trickled down Tom's cheeks. He stood up, wiped his face, and ran out of the classroom as Glen, Dean, and I watched motionlessly. Just then, Mr. Larson turned around to address the class.

"Oh darn, only five minutes of class left. I suppose you can go. I will save the trivia for next year's class. Have a great…."

No one heard the remainder of what he had to say because when Mr. Larson said "you can go" people just grabbed their things and bolted. The three of us, however, hadn't moved. Tom's words were still ringing in my ears—*what did they mean?* The next thing I knew, Mr. Larson was standing next to us, holding something behind his back. He was smiling.

"Shame I didn't get to give this to your entire group."

He produced the video tape containing our original footage from the project.

"I wanted to thank your group again for such a *marvelous* job well done. Samantha's performance, and the twist at the end—just *magnificent*. I'm so proud to be your teacher. Also, the technician at Radio Shack was able to retrieve your tape from the broken camcorder, and I viewed it. It was… much different than what I was expecting," he said.

"Uh, yeah… we, uh, decided to, uh, go in a different direction I guess," I stammered.

"*That* is an understatement, Mr. Harding," Mr. Larson chuckled. "But this first recording was also spectacular. I believe you boys and the other two are extremely gifted with your filmmaking skills. I wonder if you might be interested in submitting something for the summer film festival?"

"The what?!" we said in unison.

"Oh yes, you must. I am on the planning committee for the county film festival, and this year we thought it would be fun to include an "18 and under" category. You really ought to submit something. I think what you've already produced with your original project would put you in the running for an award. Polish it up and I bet you have a *great* chance to win. The top prize for youth submissions is $500."

"Holy shit," Glen blurted. Mr. Larson blushed but chose to ignore Glen's vulgarity.

I had spent an entire year brown-nosing Mr. Larson so that he would let me off the hook with Simon, and he did. Now he was offering us the chance to make five hundred dollars because he believed in me—*in us*. Mr. Larson was turning out to be way cooler than I originally thought.

"School is out for the summer. I've included the details on this note. I hope to see you submit something!"

***

Two days had passed, and Dean, Glen, and I were together for the first time since school let out.

"What a shitty way to end things. I shouldn't have let you guys rile me up like that," Glen said.

"Yeah, I'm sorry I snatched the phone number from Tom. I don't know what got into me. Jacob has been extra mean lately, and when I saw that number on the piece of paper, something snapped. I was going to show it to him to prove I was making progress with girls," Dean said, looking ashamed.

It was my turn to apologize, "Nah guys, it's my fault. I was jealous of Tom—I saw Samantha give him a look the other day and—"

"Oh yeah, I saw that too," Dean interrupted.

"But now I just don't know which way is up because of what he said before he stormed out. Do you guys think Tom might be, *you know*…?" I asked, my voice hushed.

"He might be *what*, Steve?" Glen asked, daring me to say the word.

"Gay," Dean whispered, as if Glen wasn't tracking.

I nodded.

"Ah. So *that's* what's been bothering you two?"

"Yeah," Dean and I said without looking at Glen.

"Look, maybe he is and maybe he isn't—what does it matter? Tom is our *friend*. He's a great guy. And I feel terrible that we screwed things up so royally with his dad that we can't even see Tom anymore. Everyone thinks Tom is so *perfect*, but he's clearly got lots going on between those perfect ears of his," Glen said with a sigh.

"I know, man. *I know*. I just feel blindsided. And I'm also wondering if Tom has the hots for me. You heard him, he said he didn't know if he liked girls 'that way' and that *I* was his first choice for the project. *Me*," I said, feeling a little awkward but needing to keep sharing my thoughts.

"That doesn't mean anything, Steve. Think about it—has Tom acted in *any* way that's made you uncomfortable? I mean, you and I have been smacking each other *in the nuts*! Does that make us gay, too?"

I had to stop and think. Before Glen started talking, I was certain I was only interested in girls. Now thinking about our ongoing game of Nut Tap had dropped me a full percentage point to only ninety nine percent sure. And with each successive recollection of us taking a shot to our dongs from the last week, my certainty decreased. Tom, however, had not laid a hand on me other than our staged fight—the same fight when he and I were wrestling each other before he accidentally punched me in the face. I exhaled slowly and looked up at Glen. He was waiting patiently for my reply, used to my tendency to work through logical scenarios slowly before answering.

"Honestly, why is this such a big deal? Who cares?" Glen said, visibly agitated.

"Well, maybe we *should* care, Glen. Being gay isn't exactly something most people are cool with, you know," Dean said.

"Yeah, whenever being gay comes up, adults change the subject and people our age get all weird and quiet—or they get mean and nasty. It sure seems like it's a *problem*—something you're supposed to hide, you know?" I said to Dean.

Glen wasn't done preaching to us yet. He stood up and ran his hands through his hair, a tick he had that usually meant he was upset about something. I braced myself.

"I guess I don't see how it's such a problem. I just don't. The only reason people react like that is because it's *different*. Are we really supposed to believe that God hates gay people, like what all those angry Christians yell on street corners? That's one of the reasons why my dad can't stand religion, by the way. After the sleepover at Tom's and going to his church and listening to Mr. Edison's surprisingly cool sermon, I asked my dad what *he* thought about Jesus, and do you know what he told me? He said, 'it's not Jesus I have a problem with—but all the hypocrites who worship him.'

So, just cool your jets and let Tom be who he is without freaking out. Dude has enough to deal with right now. I mean, how do you think *Tom* feels? His dad is a pastor! And his mom sure seems like a barrel of laughs. What do you think *they* would think if Tom told them he was gay? Maybe they'd be fine with it, but something tells me Tom is so private because he thinks that if he was found out, he'd be in deep shit— all because he doesn't know how he feels about *girls*? If Tom could get in trouble for that, then I think my dad is right. Ahh, it's all so dumb. All I know is that Tom Edison turned out to be an awesome guy—a dude we *should* be hanging out with right now."

Glen sighed and shook his head and then sat

down in a huff. Dean and I looked at him sheepishly. He avoided our eye contact, obviously ready to move on.

Once again, Glen spoke the truth. He said exactly what needed to be said and did so at the exact moment when Dean and I needed to hear them. The fact of the matter was that the *one guy* Samantha gave her number to had been the *one guy* I knew was the least likely to use it in the way *I* wanted to. And Glen was dead on; Tom wasn't some classmate we didn't know anything about anymore, *he was our friend,* and we all liked him a lot. I didn't know if being Tom's first choice meant that he had a crush on me, but after realizing the kinds of things he must have been wrestling with because of how he felt—or didn't feel—about girls, I decided to let it go. Besides, I wouldn't want Samantha or Victoria to be uncomfortable if they found out I had a crush on them, so I shouldn't feel that way if someone had a crush on me either. In the end, Glen was right, Tom deserved better than how we had treated him—plus, it felt like he really needed friends, now more than ever.

"Let's call Samantha and give her the scoop. As much as you two want to get in her pants, she is our friend now, too, and I think we should include her in our plans for the $500 that we are *definitely* going to win," Glen said as he reached for the phone.

***

We met Samantha at our school's baseball

diamond and brought her up to speed about the film contest. We left out the fight we'd had about her, and that Tom might not exactly *want* to hang out with us right now after how we had talked to him; we just said that we hoped Mr. Edison would relent and let Tom hang out with us again.

"I'm sure things will blow over with Tom's parents soon. Things will work out! But you guys, my dad totally has a camcorder, so you should have just asked, and we could have avoided this whole thing," said Samantha.

We kicked ourselves for not asking her—and Dean and I were thankful Glen was merciful enough not to say, "I told you so."

In the aftermath of our fight at school I had started to think about ways to make up for what we had done to destroy Mr. Edison's trust. I was also lost in thought about what to do for the film contest. Mr. Larson had encouraged us to submit the original project footage, and that *had* been our initial plan… until a different plan materialized in my mind's eye that could possibly solve *both* of our quandaries.

"So, I was thinking we could make our movie for the film contest about… Jesus," I said.

The three of them looked at each other and back at me.

"Mr. Edison is a pastor and he preached about how his favorite story from the Bible was the one where Jesus and Peter walked on water. I think we should make a movie about that, and then get it in Mr.

Edison's hands so—"

"—so that he will forgive us and let us all hang out again? Brilliant, Steve," Glen said, punching my arm and making me wince.

"Yeah, something like that," I said, trying to rub the pain away.

"Yeah, that sounds good to me too, Steve-o," said Dean.

"Me too," Samantha said.

"Cool. I figured we could do the walking on water scene at your house, Samantha—wondering if we could use your boat?"

"I'll check with my dad, but I think that would be okay," she said.

"I thought I would primarily work behind the camcorder this time. I was thinking Dean for Jesus, naturally, and Glen for Peter."

"Whoa, whoa, whoa. What's that supposed to mean?" Dean asked.

"Jesus was Jewish. Unless you'd prefer to *only* be a Nazi in our productions?" I asked, trying not to smile.

"Yeah, yeah. Okay," Dean said.

"And I get to play another Peter!" Glen joyfully exclaimed.

"More like play *with* another peter," I mumbled to Dean, who broke out laughing hysterically.

"Ha ha, I heard that," Glen said.

"What about me? Who do you need me to

play?" Samantha asked.

"Well, about that… there aren't many female parts in the Bible stories, unless you're okay with being Mary—who was somehow both a virgin and a prostitute?" I said without making eye contact.

"No, dumbass. There are *two* Mary's. One was a virgin, and one was a demon-possessed prostitute—or wait… maybe there were three?" Glen said, his confidence waning by the end of his retort.

"Whoa, look out, Mr. Bible is here!" Dean said as he poked at Glen's ribs.

"I was reading it the other day, bite me," Glen said as he dodged Dean's finger.

"So, which one do you prefer? The one who *never* had sex, or the one who had *lots* of sex?" Samantha asked.

Dean, Glen, and I stared at her wide eyed and paralyzed. She stared back without flinching and then burst into laughter, causing us to lose our minds, too.

"How about you play the one with all the demons?" I asked.

Samantha agreed and we continued to plot our award-winning, moviemaking Biblical masterpiece.

***

Production had stalled. We were having difficulty figuring out how to walk on water. It turns out that Jesus's miraculous stroll upon the waves was much harder to replicate than we thought it would be.

We tried using rope and had Dean and Glen do a tightrope walk to each other—which was a colossal failure. We also tried having them stand on lifejackets, which was another failure. Entering our fifth day, we decided we needed to ask for outside help.

"You know who would probably have some great ideas about this?" Glen asked.

"Glen, we've been over this. Tom is grounded. We decided we were going to make the movie and show it to Mr. Edison to redeem ourselves, remember?" I reminded.

"Yeah, we can't get to Tom until we go through his dad first," Dean added.

"Well, then, why don't we?" Glen asked.

"Why don't we, *what*?" Dean replied, confused.

"Why don't we ask Tom's dad for help—he sure seems pretty handy, what with the model taking up half his basement and all," Glen clarified.

We had intended to impress Tom's dad with the finished product of the walking on water scene. I wasn't in favor of breaking from that plan, but it seemed we had no choice.

"I hate it when you're right," I said to Glen. "We're not going to figure this out on our own. Let's call his dad and apologize and see if he'd be at all interested in helping us."

"That's what I'm talking about!" Glen shouted.

I called the Edison's and Tom's mom answered. She was not very sympathetic but said she "would run it by Mr. Edison and then let us know." I knew avoidance when I heard it as that was a tactic I used often. But then, Mr. Edison came on the line.

"Hello?"

"Hi Mr. Edison, this is Steve Harding, Tom's friend from school. Um, we're really sorry about what happened. It's not Tom's fault. It was our idea," I said.

"That's very thoughtful and brave of you to reach out and apologize, Steve."

"Yeah, um, thanks. We really miss seeing Tom. We'd love to be able to have his help with ah, ah…." I started having second thoughts about telling him our plans, worried he would see what we were up to and think I was lying to him.

"With what?" he asked, interrupting my runaway anxieties.

"With a new movie we're making. It's for the county film contest."

"Sounds interesting. But I don't think Tom's finished with his grounding yet. We were very disappointed that he lied to us."

"Yeah, okay. Sorry. Can you tell him I – we – said hi?" I said, ready to hang up and get on with my life, knowing I'd apologized and tried to help my friend.

"I will. Thanks for calling. And I accept your apology. Out of curiosity, what are you making your movie about this time?"

I felt a renewed sense of hope.

"Jesus... *sir.*" I hoped the term of respect for my elders would disarm him. It worked.

"Say again? Did you say you were making a movie about *Jesus*?"

"Yes! And we are kind of stuck and we were hoping Tom could help us with one of our scenes— the one where Jesus and Peter walk on water. I really liked how you talked about it when we visited your church."

There was a pause on the other end of the line.

"That sounds… well, that sounds *very* interesting, Steve. I–I think maybe you've discovered a way to free Tom, after all."

Mr. Edison put the phone down and I heard him walking down the hall toward the basement steps. I heard him call down for Tom to come up the stairs. More silence. Then approaching footsteps as I heard our friend emerging from the basement. There was some whispering between them that I couldn't quite decipher. Then the sound of the phone being lifted.

"Steve?" Tom asked.

"Tom!"

"What's up? You're making a movie about Jesus?!"

"Yeah man. We are. We could use your help. And maybe your dad's help, too."

***

It was great having Tom around again. We didn't speak about our argument from the last day of school, but I hoped that by reaching out to him and making things right with his folks, that he understood how we valued him and his friendship. And Glen was right, Tom's dad proved to be an invaluable source of ideas. He was even gracious about our failed attempts before showcasing his mad engineering skills that produced two walking-on-water platforms. He had figured out how to make the same thing many years ago for a reenactment that took place at a Bible Camp. I'm still not sure how it worked, but he constructed these platforms using PVC, plywood, and the material from fun noodles to create lots of buoyancy, so that when a person stood on one, the platform would dip just below the surface and still support the person's weight. The result was the illusion of standing atop the water. Having solved that problem, we deliberated about Tom's role for the movie.

"How about Judas?" I asked.

"No way, I can't let my parents see me playing the role of the biggest traitor of all time," Tom fired back.

"We need a villain though, because our movie lacks one," Dean said.

"I guess I could be one of the Roman soldiers; they weren't super popular with Jesus's people back then," Tom offered.

"Yes! Perfect!" I yelled. "You can taunt and bully Jesus and his disciples!"

"Uh, I don't know about that, but I can try," Tom said hesitantly.

"C'mon Tom, this is a great opportunity to do some *real* acting," said Glen.

"Yeah, ok, sure," Tom replied, cautiously upbeat.

***

That night, I had Glen, Dean, and Tom over for supper. I was feeling excited to have Tom back with us, and for finally figuring out how to walk on water—or at least stand on it. While we were hanging out and discussing other production details, Tom mentioned that Victoria asked about me when he was at church the other day. My stomach tumbled a little, but I managed to keep myself from falling over with joy.

"Yeah, I think she really likes you. She didn't say that, but she was wondering if she and the other two girls might be able to be in our movie, too."

"What did you tell her? You know, about being in the movie?" I said as suavely as possible.

"I told her that was fine by me. It is, right? They *can* be in it?"

"Yes! Of course. Maybe they can be Jesus's entourage of disciples or something," I said.

"Yeah, that's a great idea. Here's her number. Why don't you call and tell her yourself?" Tom handed me a piece of paper with the phone number and then quickly walked ahead of me toward the dining room for supper.

If Tom had a crush on me, he had a funny way of showing it; I didn't think he'd be putting me and his friend Victoria in touch if he wanted me in that way for himself. I decided that whether he liked me like that or not, I wasn't going to worry about it, or think weirdly of Tom. Glen's words repeated in my head: "Let Tom be who he is without freaking out. Dude has enough to deal with right now."

At supper that night, I was overcome with curiosity about Victoria, and wondered how I would sound when talking to her on the phone. My thoughts started swirling, and I was having a hard time concentrating on the meal.

"Hey Steve, you're pretty quiet over there. You okay?" Jessica asked.

Glen, Dean, and Tom all stopped eating and looked over at me. I knew I was probably going to regret cashing in on my sister's offer for free girl advice in front of my friends and parents, but I couldn't stand not knowing a second longer.

"How do I know if a girl likes me?" I blurted.

Glen, Dean, and Tom, all shot me incredulous looks. My dad started laughing. My mom stifled a giggle, too. Jessica looked at me for what felt like a thousand seconds before answering.

"Does she go out of her way to touch you when you're around her? Does she ask about you when you're not around?" she asked.

Oh my God. Victoria liked me.

"More importantly, why do you ask?" Jessica asked.

"Ah, well, I think one of Tom's friends likes me. You know, *likes me* likes me," I fumbled out.

Somehow Glen caught my attention when no one else was looking in his direction. While everyone else went back for another bite of their food, he inserted the back of his spoon into and out of his closed fist and then rolled his eyes back into his head. My milk almost went through my nose.

"And how do *you* feel about her, Steve?" asked my dad.

"Good. She's cool," I answered.

"Try not to think so much about it when you're around her, okay? If she already likes you, you've got nothing else to prove," Jessica added nonchalantly.

"So, Jessica, my love?" Glen piped. "What's this I hear about you calling me a *pervert* when I wasn't around the other day? And do you not *always* go out of your way to shove me aside whenever you see me coming? Shall I get down on one knee *now*, or wait until dessert?" Glen asked.

"Get bent! Ugh. You are the worst," Jessica said as we all lost ourselves in a fit of laughter.

*****

We finally found a day to get everyone together to shoot the scene of Jesus healing Mary of the seven demons. Victoria made it abundantly clear how she felt about me within the first five minutes of arriving. She raced up to me and held onto my elbow for support as she bent down to tie her shoelaces. Both Dean and Glen witnessed this unusual greeting and immediately began making sexual hip thrusts in the air and obscene gestures with their hands. They abruptly stopped when the other two girls looked in their direction. I was shaking silently with laughter. The girls rolled their eyes and turned their backs to them. The gestures immediately started again. It went on like this until Victoria finished tying her shoes.

"So, what's the scene? What do I need to know? Where do you want me?" Victoria asked.   I heard Glen and Dean burst into laughter, and I had to use every ounce of restraint to avoid looking at them, curious as I was to see what they were gesturing.

"You and Glen and the other disciples will walk in behind Dean, *who should be finished changing into his clothes any minute now.*"

At mention of this, Dean's eyes grew wide, and he ran into the house. I was feeling the butterflies in my belly with Victoria standing inches away, but her presence had a different effect on me than Samantha's. Something about Victoria was soothing. When I was with her I didn't temporarily black out whenever she looked at me, as was prone to happen when I was with Samantha.

I really liked being around both, but when I was with Victoria, the feeling inside was more like an exciting day of sailing versus holding onto the side of the boat for dear life. Besides, ever since she did her monologue of Anne Frank, I had started to see flashes of my sister in Samantha. Both Samantha and Jessica had this X factor when it came to how they carried themselves, both on stage and off. And even though I never, ever, thought of my sister in the same way as I did Samantha, I could see that they were the kind of girls who didn't abuse their looks or popularity by being mean. I was growing more content with thinking of her as my friend rather than as my dream girl. In the not-too-distant past I would have done anything to make out with Samantha, but there was something about her now that felt more like a sister to me.

Of course, I wanted to impress my buddies by getting the dream girl, like the heroes from the movies did, but Samantha's friendship became more attractive to me as time passed. Surprising even myself, the shift in mindset about her boosted my self-confidence and released an enormous amount of stress from my life. Freeing myself from constantly trying to impress Samantha was one of the best feelings I experienced all summer. She didn't stop being a smoke show, mind you, but all that lusting after her waned enough that I could finally function like a normal human being again—until of course, Victoria was present. I still very much wanted *someone* of the opposite gender to get to know.

Set free of my infatuation with Samantha, I decided to go after Victoria, who I was pretty certain had the hots for me. Plus, Victoria was as cute as Samantha, if not even more so, especially when those eyes of hers pierced me like they did. Every time she looked at me, I felt my face flush with warmth as everything below the waist quivered.

But shifting to friend-mode with Samantha wasn't nearly as challenging as tolerating Dean, who clearly had zero intentions of giving up his pursuit. He constantly shared with me one-liners and other ways he intended to win over her affections. I didn't dare tell him that I wasn't going to pursue Samantha any longer. I kept my thoughts to myself because he would have become a hundred times more obnoxious the instant he learned I was tapping out.

Dean obsessively and jealously analyzed her every look, touch, and comment with scientific fervor, eager to discern signs of flirtation—whether those actions were toward him, me, or anyone else. Despite how I was feeling toward Victoria, there was a part of me that felt oddly protective of Samantha; to the point that I wanted to see her end up with anybody *but* my best friend, even if that person was me, just so I wouldn't have to listen to him gush about her all day everyday. Instead, I did my best to tune him out whenever he started talking about Samantha strategies.

The first time it occurred to me that Samantha

might be more of a friend than an object of desire was during her performance as Anne Frank. While that incident gave *me* pause and made me think twice about her as a person, I'm pretty sure for Dean it was merely a free-for-all opportunity to stare at her from head to toe without consequences. I couldn't really blame him, because up until that point, Samantha had been unknown to us. We were so focused on other things that we didn't bother getting to know her. Her performance as Anne Frank, however, knocked me over the head so hard that I couldn't go back to how I saw her before.

From that point on I consciously tried to create space for her to contribute to our conversations. I let Dean interpret my actions as over the top flirting, but I was genuinely interested in what else I had missed while I had been fantasizing about marrying her and trying to start a family together.

And then there was the day we were brainstorming how to walk on water before Tom rejoined us. A conversation sprung organically, and after several spontaneous outbursts of laughter faded, Samantha suddenly started to talk our ears off.

"You guys are so much more fun than my other friends."

"No, *really*? Belinda Bowers sure seems like a laugh riot," Glen deadpanned snidely.

"Yeah, I know. *She* sure thinks she's funny," she said, her eyes dropping to her feet.

There was a moment of silence. I could see

Dean inching ever so subtly in her direction, no doubt trying to invade her personal space without being detected. Upon spotting this, Steve the Protector came to life, and all I wanted was for Dean to recognize that there was more to Samantha than a flawless complexion and mystifying curves.

"It's like I am always having to watch what I say around her. She gets off on being so mean, just waiting to pounce and show how tough she is," Samantha continued.

"Oh, she's sooo tough making fun of Simon, as if he has any choice about his condition," I said.

"Exactly! When she said that the other day, I wanted to hit her, Steve. And then when she suggested you and I were a thing? I thought about putting my arm around you, just to see what she would do."

Glen, Samantha, and I burst into laughter while Dean's face turned a shade of red I'd never seen before. His shoulders slumped and he stopped his stealthy encroachment toward Samantha. He recovered quickly though, joining in the laughter a few seconds late, with only me having noticed.

"Yeah, we all know you've got the hots for Tom though, right?" Glen asked, slicing through the commotion.

Samantha blushed and looked sideways at the three of us.

"Well, kind of, yeah, I guess," she stammered. "He's cute and all, but honestly, he was my first choice for the project because he's the only boy in our class who doesn't ogle me," her voice faded to a whisper, and she averted her eyes to the ceiling.

At mention of this, Dean and I locked eyes and grew very quiet. Quickly finding his voice again, Dean changed the subject, confidently asking:

"Do you think you'll try out for any plays in high school? You're a great actress."

"Oh yes! I love it! I hope I get speaking parts, but I'd really take anything—it's so fun to step into someone else's shoes and pretend. Isn't that why you guys love making movies so much?"

"No, I'm only in it for the money," Glen replied, laughing at his own joke before he could finish saying it.

Our time of deep conversation passed, and we returned to joking with each other and talking about our latest movie project. After a time, Glen and Dean retreated and Samantha walked over to me and put her arm around my neck and left it to rest on my shoulders. I glanced to where the guys were, and seeing the coast was clear, I relaxed. I felt as if she somehow knew I thought of her differently. Even though just seconds ago she had busted me about my unwholesome thoughts about her, I was certain she must have detected my recent change of heart.

"So do you think you could introduce me to your sister?"

"Jessica?" I asked, as if I had another sister she didn't know about.

"Yes! She's like my idol. I only have next year to share the stage before she graduates. Nothing fazes her! I want to know how she does it," she said.

I held my tongue, not wanting to divulge my sister's secret, which directly involved me and my "terrible" music. I joked with her that she would "owe me one" when I introduced her—just as my sister and I had made a similar deal. I had no idea what I would ask Samantha for but figured it would be good to have the option at the ready. She squealed happily and squeezed me in a side hug, then took her arm back and we shook hands.

"Deal," she said.

That conversation took place about a week before we started shooting, and now here we were, making our Jesus movie, beginning with *my friend* Samantha's role as the demon-possessed Mary. I was eager to see how she would respond to my directorial suggestions and what she would bring to the role herself.

I snapped back to the moment as Dean emerged from Tom's house dressed in a white bath robe, the closest imitation he could find to a first century tunic. I got the disciples and myself into position and gave Samantha the signal that we were about to start.

"Action!" I called.

I captured Dean and his disciples walking along mumbling about the weather and anything else mundane they could think of—a technique I heard Hollywood actors used to give the appearance they're talking to each other without saying anything that might take away from the scene.

Suddenly, Mary (Samantha) ran out from around the corner, shrieking and pulling her hair, then flailing her arms wildly—all Samantha's ideas. I stopped recording just as Dean and the others busted out laughing. We all got the laughter out of our systems, then resumed recording. It took us a few more takes to stop breaking character at Samantha's craziness, but eventually Dean instructed his followers to stay where they were and approached the demon-possessed Mary. Samantha continued to scream and yell and flail her arms. Dean ducked, narrowly missing several close calls to his face and body. And then he loudly proclaimed some gibberish that was supposed to be Aramaic-sounding, which Tom informed us was the language Jesus had spoken. Again, I managed to stop recording just before we all broke out in hysterical laughter. It once again took us a few takes to get past Samantha's flailing arms and Dean's gibberish without laughing.

Next, Jesus was supposed to heal the possessed woman by touching her arm. But when Dean reached out for Samantha's arm, she flinched, and he missed completely—and squeezed her left breast instead—getting to second base faster than he could have in his wildest dreams. I was unable to stop recording and we ended up having at least five minutes of uproarious laughter on tape. It took us a good long while to resume after that mishap. By the time we finally captured a usable take it was too late to incorporate Tom as the bullying Roman soldier, so we scrapped it and promised to come up with a different way to include him.

***

After Victoria and the other girls left, the five of us were sitting on the ground, laughing about the craziness of the day.

"I've been thinking," Dean said the way he did when another fantastic "idea storm" was brewing.

"Oh boy," I said, looking at Glen and Tom with a smirk. Samantha tilted her head to the side and gave Dean her full attention, too.

"Did Jesus ever get into a fist fight with anyone?" Dean asked.

"Uh, not that I know of," said Tom.

"Well, since this isn't a class project and we aren't being graded on historical accuracy, wouldn't it be cool to add a fight scene to our movie?"

The four of us looked at Dean and then at each other, all thinking deeply about his logic.

"Didn't Jesus storm a temple or something?" I asked, a vague memory of a Bible story about Jesus being angry popping into my head.

"Yeah, yeah *he did*! He was mad about people selling stuff around the temple in Jerusalem—he made this whip and overturned some tables," Tom said with excitement as Dean, Glen, and I perked up at the mention of a whip.

Tom's acumen for the Bible was coming in handy. My knowledge was vague at best. Tom's knowledge was on a different level. We watched him as he pondered Dean's question.

"Let's do it," Tom blurted.

We nodded our heads in agreement as our minds ran away with the possibilities.

"Do you think we could—" I started to say, thinking out loud, but stopped myself short, as the idea of putting Tom on the spot again felt unfair.

"Say it dude, no idea is dumb when brainstorming—didn't you tell me that once?" Glen said.

"Well, we don't have access to a temple. But being as Tom's *dad* works at a church… I don't know if he's going to want to let us do anything after what happened with our project, but, I mean, your church would make for a way better setting than my church would.…"

"Oh my god, that's brilliant, Steve!" Dean exclaimed. "We'll set up some tables and chairs and – and – and –"

"And what? *Go crazy?*" Tom asked wide-eyed. After a few moments' pause, he smiled.

We looked at each other, ecstasy bubbling just under the surface.

"We've got all the fight moves choreographed already. And who knows, maybe Jesus did take on some dudes and… that's it! *That* can be your scene, Tom! Your Roman soldier character can come in and try to stop Jesus—and then you and me can get into it!" Dean said breathlessly, barely keeping up with his runaway imagination.

"Jesus duking it out with a soldier, I like the sound of it, but I feel like there would be more soldiers hanging around," I said.

"Yeah, Steve's right. If we want to convince people that Jesus was a badass hero, then he needs to overcome unfavorable odds," said Glen.

"But the only soldier we have is *me*, right?" asked Tom.

"I can see if Barry and his friend want to help out again," Samantha offered.

We pondered silently, and then agreed—those two had kicked ass with their "stuntman" moves, and that would more than double the number of our soldiers.

"That would give us three for Jesus to overcome, but they're not very intimidating-looking though," Dean added.

And then another solution danced in my mind's eye.

"Yes, but I think I know one more sidekick to join them who is," I teased.

***

Tom's dad was surprisingly agreeable to

letting us record at his church; we didn't have much of a backup plan if he wasn't, so we were super thankful. We all piled out of the Edison's car, eager for him to open the church building so we could start schlepping tables out on the lawn. It was a weekday and not too many other people were around. Mr. Edison smiled and accepted our thanks, and then reached into his pocket and handed a key to Tom before heading in a different direction.

"I will be in my office if you need anything. Try not to break any tables, ok?" Mr. Edison was amazingly calm considering he'd just given his son and his buddies unsupervised access to *The House of the Lord*.

"Wow, he sure seems to be cool with all this," Glen said as we started walking.

"I think he digs it that we're making a movie about Jesus," Tom said. "And I think he's really warming up to you guys."

"Well, he might regret that once he sees how inaccurate we are," Glen said, laughing to himself.

"Nah, he'll be cool with it. It's my mom who is going to hate it. But dad will help her come around," Tom said.

We all brought as many board games as possible, especially ones like *Monopoly* which had fake money so we could dress the tables with plenty of props to send flying when Dean, our Jesus, overturned them. I was evaluating the state of the tables when someone tapped me on the shoulder. It was Samantha.

"Can I talk to you for a second, Steve?"

"Sure!" I said, my voice squeaking. *Damn puberty making its presence known at all the wrong times.*

She walked a few yards away and I followed her, my heartrate quadrupling with each step. I was certain I was going to die of a heart attack if she walked us out of view of the others. Dean would be sure to think we were up to something.

"I wanted to thank you for the other day—that was so fun, acting like a possessed person," she said, giggling and smiling broadly.

All I could do was nod and smile as my insides churned. I had to focus on her forehead to keep from passing out.

"I'm still new at – at being so free to – to have so much *fun* around people. And I guess I just wanted to let you know that I think you're doing an amazing job as our director. I didn't want to say that in front of the others because—"

"Thanks, Samantha. I, uh, um, that means a lot coming from you," I said and instantly broke out into a feverish sweat because of adding 'coming from you.'

She smiled. *Oh, dear god, she is just so damn beautiful.* And then it hit me again how she wasn't just a pretty face. She was also just a really, really, kind and thoughtful person—and friend. It might take me a little time, but I was slowly getting the hang of remembering that Samantha was my friend now too. The old instincts were still there, but I was reigning myself in and mastering myself more quickly each time we hung out.

"You're a terrific actress and I, uh—I'm so happy you took a chance on us and this movie and stuff," I stammered.

"Thanks, Steve," she said softly, blushing.

I didn't know what else to do, so I reached out and patted her on the shoulder and said, "no problem," and then turned to walk back to the group, knowing full well Dean's eyes had been boring a hole into the back of my skull this entire conversation. Samantha caught up to me and as we were walking side by side toward the others, she turned her head and put her hand by her mouth to whisper into my ear. My skin broke out into goosebumps.

"Victoria has a thing for you. You should ask her out."

And then, just like that, Samantha ran ahead, and the moment between us had ended. I was surprised that she said that, but not altogether shocked. I felt honored that she would confide such a thing to me about another girl's feelings and, in that split-second, I *knew* everything she said was true. I *was* a great director and Victoria *did* like me. And I *was* worthy of Samantha's friendship and Victoria's affection and *by god*, I *was* going to ask Victoria out without fear of rejection. I felt empowered and determined to finish the movie and take home the top prize. And that's when I spotted Simon aka "Shorty" approaching us in the distance, and felt my balls enlarge and chest hairs sprout. *It was directing time.*

"What was *that*? Are you two going out now?" Dean grilled.

"Oh that? That was nothing," I said nonchalantly.

Dean pushed me and I stumbled, laughing. He was furious.

"Dude, relax. She told me I should ask Victoria out!" I hissed with restraint so no one else would hear.

Dean's face softened as it dawned on him everything that that statement meant.

"Seriously? That's what she pulled you aside to say? And—well—are you going to then?"

"Yeah, *I am*. But first, let's finish this epic scene, ok?"

"Ok! But, are you sure about this, Steve-o?" Dean whispered as Simon approached.

"Relax, it'll be fine."

Truth be told, I had no idea if it would be fine or not. But ever since that day I refused to include Simon in our class project, my conscience had not let me forget how insensitive and selfish I'd acted. I hadn't planned to make it up to him and my friends in such a dramatic fashion, but when the need arose for an intimidating soldier for our movie, I couldn't resist dialing Simon, my behemoth-sized friend, and inviting him to take part. I was also very much looking forward to being *behind* the camcorder to direct Dean as *he* entered the ring versus Tom, Barry, Barry's friend, Greg… and Simon.

*****

Ever since we had assigned Tom to be the Roman soldier, he was in our ear. He was concerned that he wouldn't be convincing enough as the bad guy—which was both funny and annoying. I asked Dean to take him under his wing and to share with Tom how his brother Jacob had treated him over the years; the torments then giving Tom inspiration for his bad-guy role. The only problem with those acting lessons was that the county film festival was "family friendly," so we weren't allowed to swear, or we would be disqualified. Jacob rarely used non-swear words toward Dean and me, so we found ourselves modifying everything we wanted Tom to say during the scene.

Aside from Tom's f-bomb at his house during our sleepover, he never swore, nor mistreated others, so he completely lacked the ability to improvise taunts. He looked visibly relieved when I reminded the gang about our inability to swear on tape. As he and the other three prepared to beat the crap out of Dean, I could see him trying to memorize the list of creative insults we'd Sharpie'd on his wrists, including: fudgeface, shiplicker, mothertucker, and basskisser.

As I readied myself for the scene, it was fun to watch the younger, smaller, Barry —our crew's unlikely new stunt coordinator, giving Simon and Tom ideas and tips for how to pummel Dean. If I'd still had the hots for his sister, there was no world in which I would have agreed to let Barry and his friend be in our movie again even to humor her. And yet, here they were, and they really did know their stuff, especially Barry. He understood his role and eagerly embraced it, and it wasn't long before he had coached Simon to the point where he and the others all appeared ready to roll.

I was also eager to test a theory about Simon that I'd been thinking about during all those times I "supervised" him. I deduced that his outbursts, though having unpredictable triggers, were likely the product of unused energy. I believed that as long as Simon was actively burning off steam, his spontaneous volatility would stay dormant. Dean was still unconvinced.

"It's just a *theory* though man—if I hit him, I mean, won't that send him into a different frame of mind?"

"What if you didn't hit him?" Glen asked, walking toward Dean and me.

"No, I know—it's a stuntman kind of hit, but you know that when the fake punches are flying, one of them is bound to hit the target—remember Tom and Steve's fight?" Dean said.

"I remember," Glen said. "But I have an idea

that could win for everyone."

Glen waved the guys, including Barry and his friend Greg, to huddle up so he could relay his plan. Victoria and Samantha were far off to our right talking, which made me both nervous and excited, and the other girls were still setting up the tables and were out of earshot.

"I've been reading that Bible you gave me, Tom, and I just read about a showdown between Jesus and the Roman soldiers in some garden or something," Glen said.

"The Garden of Gethsemane," Tom said.

"Sure," Glen replied. "Anyway, Jesus didn't fight them—he, like, said something and then they just all fell to the ground."

"Yes, yes, that's awesome," I said. "What if you guys spend a few minutes laying into Dean, pushing, punching, pummeling the hell out of him with all those moves Barry's been telling you about."

"Uh, Steve—" Dean said, glaring at me.

"Hear me out, Dean. Glen's on to something. You guys are showing him whose boss and Jesus just takes it, without fighting back. The thing is, Jesus isn't exactly the fighting type, so I like this—I think it's much more realistic," I said. "After they've laid into you for a bit and you've hit the ground, you can dramatically rise to your feet, then stick your hand out and they will all drop to the ground as you pretend like you're using—"

"The force!" Tom shouted.

We all stopped and looked at Tom, the guy who not only almost never swore, but especially never referenced something from a movie. He had just completed my sentence by recalling something from one of the greatest movies of all-time, *Star Wars*.

"Right?" Tom asked, suddenly uncertain.

"How in the world—" Dean asked.

"—did you know that, Tom?" I completed the question.

"Me and my dad just watched it. He said it was his favorite movie and the reason he got into stop-motion animation."

"Huh… cool." I was thrown off by this huge change in not only Tom, but Mr. Edison *showing Tom cool movies?!* "And yeah, exactly—I think we show Jesus basically becoming a Jedi right before our eyes; wielding the force to drop the soldiers and give his disciples and him a chance to flee."

"That way, you never have to throw a punch— you just have to take one, or um, *several*," Glen said, evading Dean's jab as he laughingly said 'several.'

"Ok, let's do this," I chirped.

I corralled the girls to update them and walked through the blow-by-blow of the scene with Dean and the soldiers. Before we got going, I pulled Simon aside for a quick word out of everyone else's earshot.

"Hey Simon, glad you could be here, man. Listen, don't be afraid to just let loose, ok? The more energy you put into this scene, the better, ok?"

"You got it, Steve. Thanks for inviting me!"

I really hoped to get most of the scene in one take because once those tables started flipping, I knew it would take forever to pick up all the props and redo all the set up. I crossed my fingers, yelled "Action!" and away we went.

Dean was followed by Samantha, Victoria, Glen, and the other girls as they went table to table, decrying the sacrilege of selling merchandise in the temple courts. Dean took out his *Indiana Jones* replica whip, and miraculously missed hitting the others; sometimes coming comically close, his would-be victims relying on acrobatics to get out of the way. After they exited the "stage," I stopped recording and got into place for the next frame: the fight scene.

"Action!"

Tom, Barry, Greg, and Simon ran into frame, and Tom yelled with full voice, "That's enough, shiplicker!"

He sounded convincing enough. Dean turned to face him, and the others lunged into full swing— and I mean *full swing*. They certainly made the action look real. It was awesome. Just as Dean had been a sport with the paintball barrage to his body, so too did he let the four of them have their way as one punch and shove after another narrowly missed… or fully landed—I honestly could not tell the difference from my vantage point. All the action looked very realistic.

I stayed safely out of range behind them. I couldn't believe my eyes—or my ears for that matter—as Tom's rage included all the words we scripted for him, plus a few "basslicker's" and "fudgetucker's" that he created in the heat of the moment. I was about to stop recording after Dean fell to the ground, when I spotted Simon's muscular arms dramatically reaching down and grabbing him. I backed up a few steps, watching Simon grab hold and hoist Dean damn near above his head—and before anyone knew what was happening, Dean's body was flung through the air, landing in a heap at my feet.

"Cut!"

I set the camcorder down and knelt beside Dean.

"Steve? Is that you?" Dean asked in a daze.

"I got it, Dean—all of it! Wow, man—it looked so amazing," I said.

Dean rolled onto his back and started laughing in that hysterical way that happens when you're exhausted and there's no other way to react. Just before the others got over to us, Dean whispered, "And that was *without* him being triggered?"

Nothing else compared to the action of their battle, but the recording of Dean's recovery was pure excellence in shot selection, if I do say so myself. I started with an extreme close-up on his shallow breathing and his eyes opening while he lifted himself into a pushup position. Next, I stood behind him as he slowly rose to his feet and zoomed in on Tom's wide-eyed expression. Finally, I put them all in one shot as Dean thrust out his hand and demonstrated Jesus's Jedi powers by leveling the soldiers to the ground into a heap. *And the Oscar for Best Director goes to….*

***

Over the next couple of days, we couldn't stop rewatching the footage from the fight scene at Tom's church. We knew we had something special and we were eager to add the final touches to the film by shooting the scene that we'd all been waiting for: Jesus and Peter walking on water. We had to do some work to set up the scene before we could start filming. First, Samantha convinced her parents to let us use their pontoon, which was tied to their dock. We were allowed to untie it and use the paddles to row it out a short way into the open water, where we dropped the anchor.

Mr. Edison had stayed after driving us over to help us set up the floating platforms. He got into the water and dove with the weights to anchor the platforms to the bottom; he also offered some advice on where to position the camera so that the viewer would be less likely to see the platforms.

"Thanks for all your help with this, Mr. Edison," I said.

"You're welcome! I'm excited to see the final product, Steve. Tom keeps coming home each day more and more excited—so the last thing I want is for this scene to go poorly," he said.

Mr. Edison stood on shore, curious to see whether the platforms would succeed. We planned to wait until the sun went down to start recording because it needed to be dark, but not too dark or we wouldn't be able to see anything. Recording in the darkness also limited the number of takes we could do, so we had to make the most of our rehearsal time. I wanted Dean and Glen to test their balance before going in costume and on camera.

"Ok, Dean, give it a try," I said.

Dean walked slowly toward the water, and the instant his foot touched it, he screamed.

"Dude, Jesus doesn't scream," I said laughing.

"He might have! Damn, its freezing!"

"Just get in the water, everyone is watching you," I hissed.

Dean glanced at Mr. Edison and fixed a look of determination on his face. The platform wobbled as he began to stand, and he immediately lost his balance, dropping into the water with a large splash. He wasted little time resetting himself. Dean was resilient, but he could not stick the landing and kept losing his balance and falling into the water. There was more screaming, but he held back from cursing, aware of Mr. Edison watching from afar, not wanting to spoil the positive momentum we had built back with Tom's religious father. Dean tried again. And again. And again. He did this another five or six tries, with each attempt going just as poorly.

"You have to engage your core!" Mr. Edison yelled.

"Yeah man, he's right," Tom said. "Use those

abs, dude."

"What abs?" Glen guffawed, eliciting an annoyed look from Dean.

On his seventh and final attempt, Dean, who was soaking head to toe, stood upon the platform and didn't fall in. He smiled at Tom and waved to Mr. Edison before giving him a thumbs up and jumping off.

"Your turn, tubby," Dean quipped to Glen and covertly gave him the bird before toweling off.

"Watch and learn, twig," Glen said with a sly smile from the pontoon.

Glen's task was slightly more difficult than Dean's. Glen had to get onto the platform from the front of the pontoon, which wasn't nearly as stable as getting on from shore. I had everyone on the boat stay very still and had Tom stand near Glen, so Glen had something to hold onto as he extended his leg toward the platform. He got his other leg on the platform and looked like he might stick it on the first try… but as soon as his full body weight was on it, he crashed into the water. The entire county, including Tom's dad *the pastor*, heard Glen's blood-curdling, "Holy *fuck* that's cold!"

We all lost ourselves in a fit of gut-busting laughter.

"Glen! You can't swear!" I yelled, anxious that Mr. Edison would be judging our every move as we sought to redeem ourselves.

"I sure as shit *can*, Steve! You aren't

recording yet, are you? Besides, you get in here and try not to curse!" Glen said through chattering teeth as he tried to climb back onto the front of the pontoon.

I really didn't want to see the displeasure on Mr. Edison's face after Glen's loud f-bomb. *What if he's so offended that he packs up and leaves, and takes Tom with?* But that was not the case. I couldn't see him right away, not because he had left, but because the guy was hunched over laughing as hard as the rest of us! It was at that moment that I changed my mind about Mr. Edison. His sermon had inspired us, he gave us a second chance with Tom, he allowed us to record a brawl on the lawn of his church, and he helped us with the platforms. And now he had earned my respect because he had a sense of humor and was seemingly cool with our penchant for vulgarity.

Glen engaged his core faster than Dean had, and therefore took fewer attempts than Dean to master his balance, and soon we were ready to do the scene for real.

It was a clear night, but by the time the sun went down it was a little choppier in the water than we hoped. We decided to shoot the scene with the dialogue first and to do the water shots after because we needed Dean and Glen dry on camera.

Our plot had strayed from the Bible with Jesus and his disciples escaping in the boat after getting away from the soldiers at the temple. But we followed the Bible's telling almost word for word in this scene.

"Look! It's a ghost!" Victoria cried, pointing

into the camcorder and towards the shore where Dean was.

I turned the camcorder around to Dean, who yelled, "Take courage! It is I! Jesus! The Jewish Messiah! Don't be afraid!"

He added the "Jewish Messiah" part, but I let it slide. It was Glen's turn now.

"Lord! If it is you, then allow me to step out of this boat and walk on the water with you!"

It was the moment of truth. Dean began walking into the water, and successfully balanced his full body on the platform, an icy look of concentration upon his face. I zoomed the camcorder out just as Glen stepped onto his platform. When, at last, both appeared to be able to stay atop their respective platforms without falling in, I held them in the viewfinder and captured the shot. Glen was supposed to count to five and then fall into the water, but he only lasted until about three. Dean was holding steady as Glen breached the surface, and cried out, "Lord, save me!"

"You of little faith, why do you doubt?" Dean said, as reached out his hand toward Glen.

I captured Glen giving Dean a look that almost made me laugh aloud. We ended the scene with a dry Dean and a soaking wet Glen climbing into the boat, and I stopped recording after the others knelt and worshipped Jesus saying, "Truly you are the Son of God."

***

Tom wasn't wrong, his dad *had* warmed up to us. He told us that we were welcome to edit our project using his equipment, and that he would teach us how. Mr. Edison also suggested that when we won the cash prize we should purchase our own moviemaking equipment, and that he had some recommendations if we were interested. We jumped at the chance to learn how to edit, eager to set our film even further apart from our competition. It was so fun learning to splice everything together and add music and titles. Every now and then I could see Mr. Edison smiling at us. I think he enjoyed watching us learn as much as we enjoyed editing.

After completing the movie, editing and all, my parents took Dean and me to Mr. Larson's office, where we handed over our finished product, entitled "The Healing Hero."

Mr. Larson looked at the title with confusion.

"We started fresh with a story of our own about Jesus," I said.

Mr. Larson looked pleased.

"I am so excited to see what you've come up with—*so* excited!"

We shared his enthusiasm; we were excited to watch it too, and on a big screen with lots of people! We didn't let anyone from our families see it before we handed it over to Mr. Larson for judging—it would be much more fun to watch the finished product all together.

In the days leading up to the premiere, we learned who some of our competition was. Apparently, Mr. Larson had encouraged all the groups to consider submitting something. The only other classmates who had taken the offer were Belinda's group. Samantha disclosed that Belinda had asked her to be in it, but she turned them down, bragging that our movie was going to be far better.

"Do you know anything else about what they were planning?" I asked Samantha.

"No—but Brittany and Belinda just want to win everything. When they found out I was working with you they probably decided to step up their efforts. I bet their parents probably did most of the work. But don't worry, they're not as talented us."

Samantha was right, I wouldn't put it past Belinda to cheat and steal the spotlight away from all our hard work. Aside from the Bowers twins, Jessica shared that she was asked by some friends to be in something too, but she declined because she didn't want to compete with us. So, we knew of at least two other submissions we were up against. I was confident, but not certain that we had enough to beat out cheaters like the Bowers family and Jessica's high school classmates. But the closer we got to the festival the less I stressed about winning, and the more I just wanted to enjoy watching our movie with our friends and families.

However, when the big day arrived, I was a nervous wreck. I really wanted to win and use the cash to get our own moviemaking gear so we could start a new project. I was afraid that I had jinxed us by already spending the money in my mind. My thoughts were so consumed with moviemaking and money that I walked around in a total fog, completely unaware of my surroundings. Somehow, I made it to the football field where we'd be screening the movies… and where I nearly ran over Victoria who was bent over tying her shoes—something she seemed to do frequently.

"Steve!" she screamed as I stopped just short of her. She stood and threw her arms around me, snapping me out of my trance.

"Hey!" I shouted as I tried to get my bearings.

"Hey back!" she said as she pulled away, smiling.

I wanted the hug to continue. I wanted to kiss her. I wanted to do so many things at that moment that I couldn't come up with a coherent sentence; all I could do was smile. I must have looked like I was on drugs—I sure felt like I was.

"Hey, uh…" I stammered, the scaredy-cat Steve in the back of my mind gaining control and sending me back to the land of dwindling self-confidence. Before I could continue, Victoria hit me with a firehose's worth of questions.

"I can't wait to see the finished product! How was the editing with Tom's dad? Did it turn out the way you wanted? Aren't you just *dying* to see it and hear who won?" she gushed. Her enthusiasm was just what I needed. It fired my pride as I pondered the journey we'd shared and the accomplishment that this movie truly was. I also remembered the tip Samantha had whispered in my ear outside Tom's church, and Jessica's advice that I had nothing else to prove with Victoria. A newer, stronger, and more courageous version of me burgeoned to life within.

"Yeah, I am pumped to see it and yes, it turned out even better than I hoped!" I took a deep breath and pushed ahead—it was now or never. "Do you want to go out with me? Like on a date? To the movies?" I said nervously but joyfully, without an ounce of self-doubt.

Her smile got bigger, if that was even possible. She was speechless, but she didn't need to speak—I knew her answer the instant those glimmering, earnest eyes met my own.

"Yes. Yes, that would be great."

"Cool, I'll call you. Tonight, after we win this thing," I declared.

Before the fireworks in my heart could explode out of my chest, I was being slapped across the back with tremendous force. I assumed I had just been attacked by Glen, but I turned to see a different behemoth: *Simon.*

"Simon!" I yelled. "How are you, buddy?"

"Hey Steve!"

Simon was wearing a vest, like something

you'd see someone at Walmart wearing. In his free hand he was holding a folding table.

"What are you doing?" I asked.

"Oh, I'm just setting up—part of my summer school responsibilities," he said.

The good vibes wave I'd been surfing changed into a flood of guilt, wiping out all the joy within. I'd made progress by including Simon in our film, but I still had some atoning to do.

I glanced back at Victoria, but she was already walking away. She turned around and waved, then motioned that she was going to head toward the bleachers. I smiled and turned back to Simon.

"Uh, man, I'm sorry you have to do summer school again. I should have talked to the principal to try to help you out," I said.

"Yeah, it sucks. But Mr. Larson got me out of doing the whole summer, as long as I helped him out with this film festival today... and if I reattached the pencil sharpener," he said.

"Whoa, good for you. That's great!"

"Yeah man, it is. But hey, between you and me... I had an episode a little bit ago. I was trying to set up this table and Belinda walked by and – and I was triggered again—" he wouldn't meet my eye, and his face had grown red. I froze, envisioning a scene of Simon bludgeoning Belinda to death.

"—and I ended up ripping a leg off this thing. Can you tell?" *Oh thank god! Belinda was awful, but death by a blunt-force table to the head wasn't something anyone deserved.*

I glanced at the table's four legs; one of them was badly duct-taped to the bottom of the table. It was *very* noticeable.

"Uh, I mean, it's a little noticeable, buddy. Maybe just try to find another table to use if you can."

"Yeah, good idea. Will do, thanks. Well, hey, I gotta get going. It was good to see you, and good luck! I hope my scene turned out ok!" he said as he continued walking toward the field.

I moved on and found Victoria sitting with her friends and Tom in the front row of the bleachers. I sat down next to Tom, who was sitting at the end. I greeted everyone and, like Victoria, the other two started to gush and rapidly ask me questions. I answered them as best as I could, and then enjoyed a moment's silence as I watched Simon on the field helping Mr. Larson put up the screen and set some folders on the table that Simon had destroyed. Victoria scooted to sit so close to me that our shoulders were touching.

I pondered again how far we had all come since the day our project was assigned. I had manipulated Mr. Larson into not pairing us with "Shorty," just to end up wanting to include him in our summer film. We'd all really done some growing up. Samantha was my friend now, and Victoria was… well, Victoria was going on a date with me! Thinking about this made me wonder if *Chosen Death* was still showing, and if she would like to go see it again so that I could actually watch it this time. Then I thought about how we had royally goofed up with Tom's dad's camera, but I was grateful for how we'd made amends with him. But then my stomach dropped as I realized I'd never made amends with Tom. If I could get over my fears of asking a girl out, then I could man-up and apologize to Tom for acting the way I did that day I pushed him too far in class.

"Hey, I'm sorry I was such a – a – *shiplicker* the other day at school," I said.

Tom laughed. "No sweat, man. But thanks," he replied.

"And I'm sorry about… about what you're, ah, going through," I added quietly.

He looked at me and smiled weakly.

"Yeah, me too. Thanks, Steve," he said. "So, what should we make next?"

I wasn't sure what to expect by bringing "it" up, but I was grateful he moved on after I acknowledged his troubles. Sometimes it helped me to have people show they cared about me by talking through stuff I was struggling with, and sometimes I preferred my friends to show their support by letting me know they were there for me but letting me bring stuff up on my own if I wanted to. I could tell that Tom wanted the latter with his smile and change of subject. He knew that I accepted him and didn't think he was weird whether he liked girls the same way that I did or not. I felt good knowing I'd apologized, confirmed my loyalty to him, and let him know that he wasn't alone if he needed someone to talk to. I was relieved we could keep going like we had before.

"I don't know what we'll make next. But the first order of business will be adding some great movies to your list! Want to come over tomorrow for a movie marathon with me and the guys?"

"Yes!"

We shared a few more laughs, reminiscing about our moviemaking escapades of the last couple of months, then spotted Glen and Dean arriving with their families. Glen and Dean made a beeline for us while their parents and Jacob made their way up the bleachers to where my parents and Jessica were sitting. Jacob appeared to be in a foul mood. He kept looking around, probably hoping not to be seen. Seeing Jessica reminded me that I still hadn't introduced her to Samantha, but Samantha hadn't arrived yet.

"Ok, ok, ok. I think we got this thing, but if we don't, we are still going to make more movies, agreed?" asked Glen, as he and Dean plopped down on the bleachers between Tom and me.

"Yeah, totally," we said in unison.

"And we don't have to make more stories about Jesus, but man oh man, I think there are some juicy plotlines we could have lots of fun with if we wanted to keep going," continued Glen.

Glen still did not consider himself a church person, but after the spectacle we'd created in Tom's church school classroom, and how much we all enjoyed Mr. Edison, he was having second thoughts about what he believed. Tom had given him one of his Bibles and Glen probably read it more than most of the churchgoers I knew, myself included. For Glen, reading the Bible was less about growing his faith IQ and more about understanding Jesus; he'd confessed that Jesus fascinated him, and he sought to understand how he ticked by reading the stories about him—even if he was still skittish about religion like his dad. Needless to say, our conversations at hang outs had become more spiritual-themed since meeting Tom, whether he was with us or not.

Even Dean, who was the most tight-lipped of all, found Glen's enthusiasm for Jesus inspiring. He still didn't enjoy giving up his Friday nights to attend temple, but whenever spiritual topics were broached, usually by Glen, Dean didn't check out. In fact, he posed some interesting questions from his Jewish perspective, which often led to us asking our parents to explain and give their viewpoint. I was giving my thoughts and beliefs about God and Jesus some deeper reflection, too. I saw endless possibilities for moviemaking, just as Glen did, and thoroughly enjoyed riffing on what was written in the Bible and giving it our own spin.

We were deep in the weeds of plots and characters when we heard Mr. Larson's booming voice crackle to life on the loudspeakers: "Everyone please find your seats, the film festival is about to begin." The big moment had come!

Samantha scooted in next to me just as the first movie began, which was the one the high schoolers had made. The opening scene featured a guy and a girl arguing about something. Samantha leaned over to me and whispered in my ear—but this time, I didn't get goosebumps.

"They should have had your sister in their movie. She would have done so much better than this," she said.

"They asked but she turned them down!" I whispered back.

"She did? Well, why didn't you have her be in *our* movie then?"

Her question startled me. I hadn't even considered asking my sister to be in our movie. Part of me wished I had because she was, after all, an incredible actress. The other part of me knew that it was better I didn't because she was my sister and having her around would have changed the dynamics of everything. It was hard to imagine me earning my stripes as a director while standing in my sister's shadow. Add to that the obnoxious version of Glen that appeared whenever Jessica was in our vicinity.

"Oops! Next time!"

The first movie submission ended, and people applauded excitedly. It was a solid, but not spectacular effort. They really needed a star, like Jessica, to give it more of an edge. I was grateful she'd declined. Mr. Larson introduced the next movie, and it was Belinda and Brittany's submission. I groaned and rolled my eyes. Samantha elbowed me in the ribs.

"Don't be a poor sport," she admonished with a wry smile.

Samantha's prediction had been correct—the movie was clearly influenced by adults. It wasn't funny despite clearly trying to be, and it came off as too polished. I could tell that they had used a teleprompter of some kind to help the twins with their lines, making their performance feel unnatural. I honestly didn't even know what the plot *was*—they spent too much time editing with fancy titles and transitions and didn't focus enough on telling a good story.

After the final credits aired, which only listed the Bowers family, people applauded, but much less enthusiastically. Our movie was the last to be shown. Thankfully, there were only three submissions, so by the time ours came up, I knew without a doubt that we were going to be $500 richer. The only way I figured we would lose was if the Bowers had bribed Mr. Larson, which Samantha said they had been successful doing with teachers in the past. If I hadn't spent so much time with Mr. Larson, I might have been more nervous—but I was one hundred percent sure he was not the bribe-taking type. We anxiously awaited the opening titles with everyone else. As the introductory music began, a hush fell over the crowd. I couldn't think of anything more enjoyable in the world, outside of a first kiss with Victoria, than watching something on the big screen that me and my friends had so much fun making.

People laughed, gasped, cheered, and were silent at all the right moments, and when the screen went black and the credits rolled, the bleachers *erupted*. My friends and I exchanged high fives as the crowd roared their approval. I stood and looked up to where my family sat and smiled as their faces beamed with pride and joy. I caught Jessica's eye and waved for her to come down to the first row.

When she arrived, I didn't even need to make the introduction—Samantha ran to greet her, and she and my sister were instantly jumping up and down, giggling and chatting like long-lost friends. Glen and Dean gaped, and I couldn't help laughing at their spectacle of lust. They were still staring when Samantha started making her way back to us. I saw Jessica catch Glen's eye as she made her way back up the steps to her seat. She smiled at him and waved, and he waved back. He later confessed that he thought he was going to pass out—which explained why he completely missed his seat and almost fell under the bleachers.

My thoughts kicked into full gear and a fun idea popped into my head. As I expected, when Jessica returned to her row, she and Jacob shared a quick exchange, and Jessica was pointing toward our group. Jacob's gaze turned our way. I tapped Samantha on the shoulder.

"Hey, I'm cashing in my favor *right now*."

"Oh? What is it?"

I whispered it in her ear. She looked at me, smiled, and then turned to Dean and planted a kiss on his cheek. She also gave him a huge hug, and then leaned her head on his shoulder. I never took my eyes off Jacob. His jaw dropped… and then his face broke into a wide grin. I looked over at Dean and saw a mirror image of his older brother's smile. He had no idea what was happening, and I didn't bother telling him—there would be time for that later. Dean deserved a surprise moment of bliss, just as he had unintentionally given me during *Chosen Death*.

Before indulging in celebration with my friends, I scanned the bleachers in search of Tom's parents. I found them looking in my direction, and just like my own family, Mr. Edison's face radiated with satisfaction and pride.

***

I had discovered my love for moviemaking, welcomed Tom into my inner circle of best friends, plus, gotten over my paralyzing fear of talking to girls. I was looking forward to all the new adventures that awaited in high school. Above all, I learned that a person was so much more than what you could see on the outside; Simon was more than his nickname and disorder, and getting to know Samantha and Tom revealed that even the people who looked to have life all figured out were every bit as human as the rest of us. Time and again throughout this experience, I'd discovered the joy of storytelling—and that the best story of them all was my own.

And as amazing as our successes were, they were a distant second to the experience of creating and sharing them with others—there was no such thing as making too many friends. I had been beginning to resent being known as "everybody's friend," but as I looked at Mr. Edison, Mr. Larson, Simon, Samantha, and even Samantha's obnoxious brother Barry, being *everybody's friend* meant something different than it did before. I now embraced my nickname, and wondered what the world would be like if *everyone* was known as *everybody's friend.*

After what felt like an eternity of cheering and celebrating the premiere of "The Healing Hero," Mr. Larson walked up to us with an enormous smile on his face and a handheld microphone in his hand. He congratulated our moviemaking crew on a job well done, then handed us the blue ribbon and an envelope with $500 inside, before walking back to the other judges. He set down the handheld microphone, and with his other hand groped for the corner of the table, then slowly began to sit down. Which gave me a split second to spot a very noticeable duct-taped table leg awaiting the brunt of his gargantuan frame. *This was it. We're about to see history.*

In one magnificent millisecond, it was over— Mr. Larson destroyed that poorly reconstructed table as he and it crashed to the ground, sending our beloved Media Arts teacher ass over teakettle just as we had all envisioned it.

"Shorty broke the leg and reattached it," I said to my friends through tear-soaked sobs of laughter.

"Still counts," said Glen.

For more information about Keith:

www.authorkeithlong.com